Princess of
Shadows

THE QUENTARIS CHRONICLES

Quentaris in Flames, Michael Pryor

Swords of Quentaris, Paul Collins

The Perfect Princess, Jenny Pausacker

The Revognase, Lucy Sussex

Beneath Quentaris, Michael Pryor

Slaves of Quentaris, Paul Collins

Stones of Quentaris, Michael Pryor

Dragonlords of Quentaris, Paul Collins

Angel Fever, Isobelle Carmody

The Ancient Hero, Sean McMullen

The Mind Master, John Heffernan

Treasure Hunters of Quentaris, Margo Lanagan

Rifts through Quentaris, Karen R. Brooks

The Plague of Quentaris, Gary Crew

The Cat Dreamer, Isobelle Carmody

Princess of Shadows, Paul Collins

Nightmare in Quentaris, Michael Pryor

The Murderers' Apprentice, Pamela Freeman

Princess of Shadows

Paul Collins

Series editors: Michael Pryor and Paul Collins

Lothian
BOOKS

To the gals at the Shepparton Library —
and warrior librarians everywhere.

Thomas C. Lothian Pty Ltd
132 Albert Road, South Melbourne, Victoria 3205
www.lothian.com.au

First published 2005

National Library of Australia
Cataloguing-in-Publication data:

Collins, Paul, 1954– .
Princess of Shadows.

ISBN 0 7344 0799 8

I. Title. (Series: Quentaris chronicles).

A823.3

Cover artwork by Marc McBride
Back cover artwork by Grant Gittus
Map by Jeremy Maitland-Smith
Original map by Marc McBride
Cover and text design by John van Loon
Printed in Australia by Griffin Press

Contents

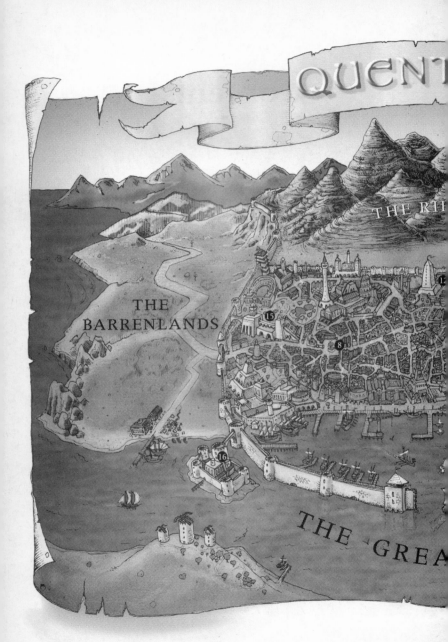

QUENT

THE RII

THE
BARRENLANDS

15

8

16

THE GREA

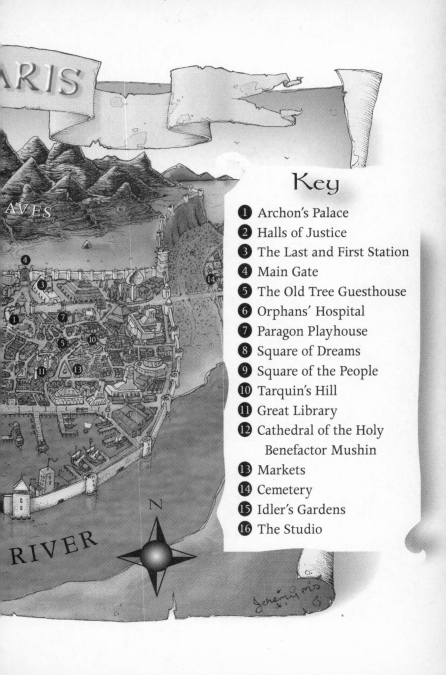

Key

1 Archon's Palace
2 Halls of Justice
3 The Last and First Station
4 Main Gate
5 The Old Tree Guesthouse
6 Orphans' Hospital
7 Paragon Playhouse
8 Square of Dreams
9 Square of the People
10 Tarquin's Hill
11 Great Library
12 Cathedral of the Holy Benefactor Mushin
13 Markets
14 Cemetery
15 Idler's Gardens
16 The Studio

Prologue

A DIZZYING HEIGHT ABOVE the cobbled streets of Quentaris, the wind hissed like a living thing, twisting tortuously around chimney and gable, seething about the ancient ornate stonework that sculpted the city's skyline. Wind and darkness overtook the city. Ragged clouds whipped across the moon's face, making shadows leap and race over the sleepy rooftops.

But not all the shadows were insubstantial.

Some creaked and groaned, unfolding slabs of darkness; limbs stretched with the grinding sound of granite. Eyes snapped open, globes of red in the night, glaring about ferociously. And voices could be heard, though none like these had ever been heard by those sleeping in the dark houses below. They were the voices of stone and canyon, like a slow churn of gravel, or the ponderous flow of lava.

The glowing eyes blinked, waking from a long sleep. But there was no satisfaction at this awakening. Rather a grim sadness.

A dozen of these shadowy figures gathered, murmuring together, then moved, swiftly despite their heavy bulk, melting into the shadows, becoming deeper chunks of shadow. They swept across rooftops, climbed down walls, invaded houses. Where they found humans sleeping, or those still awake, they touched them with cold hands before their victims could scream or snap out of their frozen horror.

With a sound like the freezing of water speeded up a thousand times, the humans turned instantly to stone.

The shadowy creatures did not tarry. They left the standing or reclining statues that once were human and sought out others, leaving behind a trail of incredible destruction, the kind that earthquakes bequeath, or that left by the rush of a mighty boulder down a mountainside.

Rift Enchantress

TAMAIKA ERSKONA TRAILED HER three plump sisters up the marble stairs of the Great Library of Quentaris. As usual, Tamaika's older sisters were bickering, their whining voices puncturing the otherwise quiet morning air.

'It's your turn to work in the cellar,' Byra said to Gabra.

Gabra bridled. 'I worked down there last week.' She turned to her other sister, Hetta. 'I don't recall *you* having worked down there in ages.'

Hetta swirled her hair loftily. 'Old Bat Tomes says I don't have to any more. I feel sickly in the damp.'

'An allergy is it?' sneered Gabra. 'An allergy to work more like it.'

There was a silence, and Tamaika's shoulders slumped automatically. She knew where this argument was heading. Although nothing her three sisters could do to her today would stifle the happiness welling up inside her. Today was different from all other days in Tamaika's life. Today was a very special day. Yet no matter what happened, it was important that Tamaika revealed nothing of this to her overbearing sisters. If they knew the truth, if they even suspected, they would mock and tease her, and do their best to destroy the seed of joy that grew as each minute passed. So she looked down at her feet, maintaining the glummest expression she could.

Her three sisters turned at the top stairs and said in unison, 'It must be Tamaika's turn for cellar duty!'

They laughed in their usual horsy buck-toothed manner and swept through the double doors, instantly cheered by their latest bit of slyness.

However, before the doors slammed shut on Tamaika's face, she saw Byra look back at her, a faint suspicion creasing her forehead. Their eyes locked and Tamaika's heart thumped. Byra arched one eyebrow. Had she guessed Tamaika's secret? Tamaika shivered at the thought.

It was the right response. Byra's face broke into a

malicious smile. She stabbed a finger toward the cellar stairs and snorted.

Tamaika dragged herself across the room and down the stairs. The dungeon, as it was known amongst the library staff, was an annexe to the Department of Cataloguing and Repair, although little cataloguing or repairing actually went on down there. No, this was where outdated titles and records, banned volumes and books damaged beyond repair (due to budget cuts), were bundled, rarely to be seen again. Much like those misfits unlucky enough to be sent there.

Tamaika lit an oil lamp and sat it in the darkest corner of the great arched cellar. Two slanting shafts of light from a grate that opened to a cobbled street high above stabbed the darkness. Noises and the faint reek of fresh horse dung drifted down to Tamaika, along with the secretive chatter of street urchins and the clatter-clank of wagon wheels. The dungeon itself projected out beneath the streets of Quentaris, in the same way that the bottom layer of a pyramid is larger than those above. But despite her virtual imprisonment here in the mouldy dungeon, Tamaika smiled to herself. Had anyone seen her, they would have been most puzzled. A smile in this place was rare enough, but the gleam of excitement in her eyes was almost shocking.

Tamaika hugged herself, thinking of her book, *Rift Enchantress*, which was due to be published today. Tibbid, the local town crier, had promised to announce its publication throughout the city. She couldn't quite believe that she was now an author. A *published* author.

She suddenly realised she'd laughed out loud and froze, listening carefully.

It was as quiet as a laden coffin in the dungeon, but Tamaika had learnt never to relax her guard. Her sisters had an uncanny knack of knowing when she was happy. If they caught even a whiff of her excitement, they would whisk her out of there to perform some onerous chore, or find some way to ruin her mood. With little to be joyous about themselves, they hated to see happiness in others, especially their younger downtrodden sister.

But she heard nothing. It seemed that she was safe from prying eyes and ears for now. Tamaika glanced over at the stairs, then went quickly to a slag heap of congealed papyrus. Pulling the mound aside, she reached behind it and pulled out an ancient book.

Positioning a chair in one of the shafts of natural light, and where she could see the top of the darkened stairwell, she sat and ran her hands over the leather-bound, gold-embossed volume.

'*Princess of Shadows*,' she said reverently. The two-thousand-year-old book felt heavy in her hands, as though it contained more than just parchment and text between the leather and wooden covers. Now there's an imagination, Tamaika laughed at herself. Quite by accident, she had discovered the long-lost book just two weeks ago, while airing a particular musty section of books high up in the shelves. She'd been scrubbing behind a bluestone column when she realised that a book had fallen down behind it. After a brief struggle, she realised the book had been hidden there deliberately, since it could not have got there otherwise. Or maybe it was magicked there, a voice inside her said. She almost laughed again. Lately her head had been full of such fanciful thinking.

She glanced nervously up at the stairs to ensure her privacy. It was her second reading of the epic, yet it may as well have been the first, such was its freshness and vision. A voracious reader, she was soon lost in realms of fantasy and adventure, dreaming of herself as the legendary Mithla, the Princess of Shadows — a heroine who loved Quentaris beyond all else and rose to its defence when all seemed lost.

Had she not been so engrossed in the book, she might have noticed her breath frosting on the air that had suddenly become chill, and a kind of thin smoke — like a ghostly presence — rise up from the ancient leaves of parchment and slowly envelop her in a sinuous vortex.

House Mercutis

CHIEF CONSTABLE CADOR MERCUTIS of the City Watch Investigators slumped behind his desk. It had been a devil of a night. Smashed statues and wrecked property he could handle. Murder and mayhem were also part of the job. But citizens turned to stone were beyond his ken. He flicked through the reports on his desk. According to Commander Storm's watchmen, squat figures had been seen stamping across the rooftops during the night. No one had got a good look at them, but most agreed that they must have been goblins.

'Invulnerable goblins,' said the famed archer Terza, who swore that he had hit one of the perpetrators dead centre with a crossbow bolt, but the bolt had shattered against it. There was much laughter at this assertion, and Terza was forced to back down, grudgingly admitting that perhaps his aim had erred slightly and he'd hit a stone pillar after all. But to himself he muttered quietly, 'Aye, a stone pillar that moved, by the gods.'

Those near enough to hear this laughed harder.

The goblins could have been armoured, Cador reasoned. That would also explain their sluggishness, for goblins were frightfully nimble.

But the goblins had a perfect alibi, as they'd explained to him when he visited their council. They hadn't left their underground grotto all night, for it had been the celebration of Good Hocking, or some such festival. Surely, he had argued, some of their number had imbibed a little too much and had been swept away beyond good cheer and reason. No, Dreepak — the goblin elder — had replied, the spirit of Good Hocking required that all brethren stay underground and *fikh*-bonded for a full twenty-four hours, from first light to last dark.

At that point the situation had almost gotten ugly, with several indignant goblins jostling his squad and jeering at them. Outnumbered and clearly in the wrong, Cador asked forgiveness for any unintended breach of the goblin truce, and retreated with all civility and haste.

The more he pondered the situation now, the more he realised he was desperately out of his depth.

If not the goblins, then whom? And even if he could attribute the wanton damage to the sometimes malicious goblins, how could he explain some of Quentaris's finest citizens being turned to stone? And why were all the victims men and women of status and wealth? Was there more to this than a simple raid? Revenge, perhaps? It was a pity his father was ailing right now, and yet Cador took grim satisfaction in knowing that he was technically only the deputy chief constable, acting in his father's stead. Responsibility was sweet, but it was a two-edged sword.

Typically, his twin brother, Maxon, was nowhere to be seen when trouble arose. Maxon's uncanny instinct, that frequently seemed to give him a fore-knowledge of disaster, had once again kept him away. Pity Cador had not been born with a similar intuitive power. He might have stayed in bed with his head firmly under the pillow.

Cador thumped the table with his fist and sighed heavily. He had not asked for this job; he had often dreamed of becoming a renegade prince instead, one of those bold and resourceful nobles — bereft of House status — who sought romance and adventure in the rift caves. Now there was a life! One without an ounce of paperwork or bureaucracy. Cador sat back and sighed, tut-tutting himself in reproach. What was he thinking? Acquiring the chief constable's job was all that had kept the Mercutis name both solvent and somewhat esteemed. His actual title — Prince Cador — was a hand-me-down from ancient times, an honorific he seldom used.

No, Cador could never become the rift cave adventurer of his dreams. The nearest he would come to that life was in reading the classics on the subject, written by the real adventurers of the world.

His lineage had indeed bequeathed him a heavy load to bear. The once proud House Mercutis had formerly been one of the most prestigious Houses in Quentaris. But a run of bad military engagements and imprudent investments had seen the House reduced in both wealth and status. Above all else Cador wanted to restore House Mercutis to its rightful place, beside those of the Duelphs and Nibhellines. He and his father had sworn on his mother's grave that they would strive to re-establish the Mercutis name. His father had almost died trying to live up to that promise. And his brother Maxon? The wastrel seemed intent on his petty political intrigues, none of which would ever amount to anything.

He reached across his desk and plucked out a book from a glass case. He had read *Peril of the Rift Caves* many times, yet he still felt the thrill of the chase within its pages. He read the frontispiece, but stopped. Staring blankly at his bookshelf, he thought back to some advice he had sought the previous night.

He had visited Nilus, the Nibhellines' mage, and then Godrund, the Duelphs' mage. Both had hinted in their usual mysterious manner that, among other things, an ancient evil was creeping across Quentaris.

'Look to the ancient scripts,' Nilus had said. 'Those who do not remember the past are condemned to relive it.'

Godrund had been just as dour. 'All is not what it seems,' he said. 'Nor is all that is writ anew to be dismissed.'

'Ancient scripts. The past. The new,' Cador murmured to himself. Replacing *Peril of the Rift Caves* he scanned the historical books in his collection.

Selecting one title that his hand strayed to, he sat back down. *The Compleat Book of Mythology and Magic* was not a book he would normally choose to read. Said to be factual, many scholars had published dissertations on how impossible some of the stories were. Why, one of the tales even maintained that the world was round, when surely any eye could see that it was curved like a great soup bowl!

Cador turned his oil lamp up and settled in for a serious read.

Cador woke with light streaming through his barred window and a town crier announcing murder most foul, a strange malady … and the publication of a great book by a first-time novelist.

Cador rubbed sleep from his eyes, and picked up *The Compleat Book of Mythology and Magic*. He must have fallen asleep while reading the tome. 'Heavy going indeed,' Cador mumbled. Still, he had learnt that, according to the book, the Hakogna, the city's ancient and weathered gargoyles, hundreds of which sat atop many a house, tenement and palace in Quentaris, rose in defence of the city once in every century or so. For a moment he had wondered if there was a way to awaken them now, when Quentaris was once again in need. 'Utter nonsense of course, but sometimes I wish …' He splashed cold water on his face from a basin, not quite sure what he wished for.

'*Rift Enchantress*!' came the voice of a town crier through Cador's open window. 'Read all about it! Romance! Adventure! Derring-do! A book for all folk, young and old, prince or pauper alike! Remember the name! Dacy Dunnard! Read it, if you dare!'

Ordinarily, Cador would have ignored the announcement of yet another racy pot-boiler from the pen of some fever-brained author, but he suddenly recalled the words of Godrund: not all that which is writ anew should be dismissed. He murmured the words aloud and they hung in the air for several long moments.

Then he clambered to his feet and with a sudden sense of urgency rushed from his office to seek out this new book by Dacy Dunnard.

3

Cador Plays a Hunch

TAMAIKA WAITED FOR AS long as she could. Although the midday bells had not pealed, she knew her book must have reached the book vendors by now. Tibbid, the town crier, had deliberately lingered by the grated apertures that fed light to the cellar and announced the publication of her *Rift Enchantress*.

Tamaika messed up her clothes, rubbed her eyes red, and immersed herself in misery. She walked stonily up the stairs, eyes downcast, lips quivering.

'There she is!' Byra bawled to the head librarian. 'I'm sorry Head Tomes, but we try to make her presentable and what not. We're at our tethers' end, aren't we, Gabra?'

'Wits' end, for sure,' Gabra called from the antiquarian aisle.

Tamaika groaned silently. She had hoped to evade her sisters at least this once. She raised her head and looked around, as though in a stupor. 'I'm sorry Byra, did you call me?'

'Tch,' Byra sneered. She bustled over, her obesity slowing her to a waddle. 'Let me straighten up your bun at least, if you're out in public.'

Tamaika allowed her hair to be pulled tighter than it needed to be and re-pinned. Byra then lightly slapped her face with both hands. 'You need a bit of colour, you do,' she said.

'Yes, well, enough of that,' Head Librarian Tomes said from the front desk. She looked down her long beak of a nose at the mousy librarian. She couldn't quite explain why, but she always felt uncomfortable around Byra's youngest sister. She was an excellent worker and never complained. She knew the place inside out, and yet there was something …

'Sorry, Head Tomes,' Byra said. 'It's just come to me. Tamaika, aren't you on dungeon, I mean, *cellar* duty? It is your shift, isn't it?' she asked pointedly.

Tamaika nodded meekly. 'It's the damp,' she said, mimicking Hetta's excuse. 'I think a little fresh air might tide me over till my duties are done.'

'A bit of fresh air, is it?' Byra scoffed. She rolled her eyes toward the ceiling for Head Librarian Tomes's benefit. '*Fresh air?*'

'You are excused,' Head Librarian Tomes said, before Byra could say another word. 'Make it brief, Tamaika. Take a drink from the fountain maybe. It will do you the world of good.'

'Off you go then,' said Byra. 'And thank Head Tomes for her generosity.' She shook her head in wonder. 'The youth of today, I don't know,' she said. 'No backbone.'

Tamaika slumped down the library's steps, crossed Wayfarer Street and dragged her feet until she was halfway across the university's grounds. Get well out of sight, her mind urged, and, unusually fleet-footed, she raced the rest of the way. Down Fences Lane, brushing past hawkers of illicit goods and straight to the book vendors in the market place.

'Dacy Dunnard?' the first book vendor repeated. 'Never heard of him.'

'Her,' Tamaika said.

'What?'

'Dacy Dunnard is a her, not a he,' Tamaika explained quietly.

'I don't care if Dacy's a donkey's rear end, miss, I

still ain't heard the name. Show me the colour of your money and I'll pick you out a good read. *Romance in Hadran* is only a couple of copper rounds. A nice book. Thoughtful.'

Tamaika turned in panic and bumped straight into a uniformed man. 'Ulp!' she yelped.

'No harm done,' the man said. He held Tamaika's shoulders, for she looked as though she was about to swoon. 'Are you feeling unwell, girl?' he asked.

'I'm just after a book,' she explained breathlessly. 'It's supposed to be on sale. I … I heard a town crier announce it,' she said in desperation.

'So did I.' Cador unwrapped a package in his hand. 'I don't suppose this is the book you're after?' he asked.

Tamaika felt dizzy and must have wilted because the next thing she knew the stranger was assisting her to the market fountain.

'Have a sip,' he said, cupping his hands to Tamaika's mouth. 'You're a waif of a girl and no mistake. And pale as fine porcelain.' He looked around as though to call for help.

'I'm fine, truly,' Tamaika said. 'In my excitement I ran all the way here, and I fear I am not at all up to such exertion. But there I go again, forgetting my manners. I'm Tamaika.'

Cador stared at her. Godrun's words came back. *Those who do not remember the past are condemned to relive it.* Intended for loftier moments, no doubt, but still there was an odd echo of the words here that made him uneasy.

'Sometimes I think my head is as solid as a rock,' Tamaika said nervously when Cador did not answer at once, but continued staring at her.

Rock, thought Cador. People are being turned into rock. Am I imagining all these references? He looked down at *Rift Enchantress*. It seemed an ordinary book, hardly one that carried within it the key to last night's rampage. But who was he fooling? No one brought up in Quentaris could doubt the first law of magic: that there are no coincidences. In his hands then, he might well hold the answer to the night-time mysteries, if he could only fathom the puzzle.

And what about the girl?

'Where is it that you purchased the book? Was it over at Tash Morley's stand?' Tamaika asked, staring in fascination at her book.

Cador snapped out of his reverie. 'Oh, sorry. Yes. Ordinarily I wouldn't contribute to that rogue's coffers, but he seems to be the only one selling it. "Purveyor of fine literature", he calls himself. That's rich.' He realised in a second that the girl might know the author, and back-pedalled. 'It's from a small press, I see. Er, do you know the writer?'

'Me? Oh goodness, no,' she said in a rush. She was feeling quite odd and wondered if she was coming down with something. Her face was flushed and she had a strange uneasiness in her stomach. She frowned. The thought of her book not being for sale must be making her feel ill. That was it. It surely couldn't have anything to do with the presence of this handsome and gallant stranger. 'Er … thank you for your assistance,' she blurted out before turning and hurrying away.

'You're welcome,' Cador responded. Before she was out of sight, he called, 'Where did you say you're from?'

'I didn't. I'm from the library,' Tamaika called back. 'I'm always at the library.'

As she ran off, she thought, now why did I tell him that?

Mithla, Arise

SQUIRRELLED SAFELY AWAY DOWN in the cellar, Tamaika fondled her new book, bursting with excitement and pride, and not a little impatience. Returning to the library all she had wanted to do was rush down to the dungeon and open the bag containing her book, but before she could do so her spiteful sisters had waylaid her.

'Had a nice break, have we?' Byra sneered as she tried to rush past them. 'In need of fresh air, huh? A likely story. You've been meeting someone. A man, no doubt. Always figured you for a trollop.'

'I had a drink at the fountain,' Tamaika said, trying to keep the package with her book out of sight, but failing miserably.

'What's that you've got there? Give us a look then,' Byra reached for it but just then Head

Librarian Tomes rushed in, glaring around.

'Come on, you lot,' she said, obviously out of patience. 'I've been calling you. Didn't you hear me? That witchling niece of Lord Chalm's has been in again. I do wish he'd control her.' She wrung her hands in frustration.

Happy to divert attention from herself, Tamaika asked quickly, 'What's she done this time?'

Head Librarian Tomes rolled her eyes. 'What hasn't she done? As if it wasn't enough to magic all the animals out of the books in the zoology section last week and have them running riot in the library and pooping everywhere. Oh, no. And obviously it wasn't sufficient entertainment last month making all the books grow teeth and try to bite customers they didn't like the smell of. No, of course not. Now she's trying to make amends. Wanted to apologise.'

'What'd she do, Head?' chorused the three sisters.

'Nothing really. Just thought she'd help us catalogue all the books in the library and reorganise them.'

Tamaika said slowly, 'Well, it is a big job and they do need reorganising.'

'By colour?'

'Pardon?'

'She organised them all by colour. Said she

thought it was much prettier than doing it by title, author and subject. So all the blue books are now together, next to the pinks, greens, reds, orange, and yellows.' She stared at them above the dark rim of her glasses. 'If any of you can come up with a way to strangle the child without upsetting his lordship, let me know. Until then, come with me.'

It took quite a while to put all the books back the way they were and they would still have been at it a week later if Head Librarian Tomes hadn't relented and agreed to hire a wizard to undo the precocious magic of the six-year-old niece of Lord Chalm.

Finally safe in the dungeon, Tamaika opened the bag and lifted out *Rift Enchantress*. The cover was as exactly as she had described it to the book's illustrator though now as she peered at it closely by lamplight, Tamaika realised the rift enchantress looked surprisingly similar to how she pictured Mithla, the Princess of Shadows: a feisty heroine in a gold trim, red cape, with rapier drawn and bent on mayhem and destruction in defence of Dmenian slaves being illegally traded by people smugglers. The look on her character's face assured the reader that no one messed with the enchantress.

No one knew that she had written the book under a pseudonym. Her sisters would have burned every page, shred by slow shred, if they had ever discovered the manuscript.

Tamaika began reading her book from page one with the intention of reading the book right through to the end. Night fell around her, and the library closed for the day. Despite not having eaten a thing all day, Tamaika felt an unusual energy building within her. She put it down to the excitement of holding a copy of her book and of having met someone who had actually paid to read the words that she had written. An educated man and from the look of him a senior officer in the constabulary.

As she read she was unaware that a quill behind her had floated off the table and started twitching, as if it was scribbling words in the air. Later, several books in different parts of the dungeon opened, one page turning at a time, as if an avid but invisible reader was reading them.

None of this Tamaika noticed. She was too engrossed in her own story.

But when she reached page one hundred and eighty-five something alarmed her and she shut the book. She looked up, expecting to see her sisters smirking down at her from the stairs. It was then that she realised that the library was closed, and that she had been locked in. She stood in fright, but a low lambent light commanded her attention. It came from behind a tottering pile of old papers. Drawn to the light, Tamaika reached behind the dank papers and pulled out the *Princess of Shadows*.

The ethereal light emanating from the book grew till it nearly blinded her. 'Oh!' she squealed and stumbled backwards. She spread her hands to balance herself, but before she knew it she was twirling around and around as though invisible hands were spinning her about.

The light enveloped her completely and became so bright that for a moment nothing — including Tamaika — could be seen within it. Wracked by pain and badly frightened, Tamaika gasped aloud, then collapsed to the ground in a heap. She stayed there for some minutes, until whatever magic had been directed at her had dissipated. She had read many books on magic and wizardry, and knew that old latent magic, or 'residuals', were lying every-where in Quentaris, waiting to trap the unwary. They accounted for many mishaps, like fires, broken household items and personal accidents. The only resistance to these forgotten traps was to give in to them and hope they had lost their power with age.

Against all odds, she realised that she had not

been a victim of latent magic. Or if she had, it had been a beneficial one. She flexed her arms and felt power in them. She took a step, but instead of her practised leaden footfall, her foot almost glided across the threadbare carpet.

Sensing a trick, Tamaika swirled around, dreading who she might find there in the dim cellar. Surely her sisters had laid a trap for her.

A metallic rustling stopped her. She looked down and stifled a gasp. Someone had dressed her in a bizarre costume. At first glance, she was wearing the same cloak that the enchantress was wearing on the cover of her book, but this one was midnight black with a blood red lining. Strapped around her waist was a belt with a rapier in a richly inscribed leather scabbard. Taut leggings rippled with muscles beneath. And despite the darkness Tamaika realised that she could see the top of the stairwell as though a torch guttered there. Further, she could hear outside noises as though she were beside them.

Before she could even begin to understand what had happened to her, a mind-jamming pain pounded in her head. From that moment on she was no longer Tamaika, Librarian Third Class; she was the newly reincarnated Mithla, Princess of Shadows.

A thousand noises bombarded her: mice and rats scrabbling about in wall cavities; light-footed thieves scampering across the rooftops; dung brigadiers sweeping the night's horse droppings and cleaning the catchments for the street sewers; people quarrelling and laughing; street vendors hawking their wares.

'Nothing changes,' she murmured to herself in a whisper. 'Yet everything changes.'

A heavy scraping noise drew her attention. Right upstairs, directly above her. Either in the main library, or on its roof.

Mithla closed her eyes, accessing Tamaika's memory. In an instant she knew where she was, what year it was and even had a suspicion as to the cause of the city's current problems. Without further thought, she rushed up the stairs. She didn't have time now to worry that her surrogate body might not be strong enough for what she had to do with it. She only knew that something was threatening Quentaris and that she had been summoned from her sleep to stop it. With this purpose consuming her, she took the stairs five at a time. She stopped at the front counter and listened, tuning into the grating noise.

'There you are,' she muttered, looking up. Within

the space of twenty heartbeats, she was on the fifth balcony, directly below the dusty dome that shed watery moonlight into the library's otherwise murky interior. There were ventilation windows up there that were opened by long poles with hooks on them. Mithla latched on to a window with a hook, opened it and lithely scaled the pole.

She had barely squeezed through the child-sized window when instinct made her drop to the shingled roof. A stone cudgel slammed into the window frame, narrowly missing her head. Shards of glass exploded and tinkled to the library's floor.

Mithla rolled, recovered her footing and drew her sword. Too late she realised the creature was not born of flesh and bone, but of granite. It wrenched its stone cudgel from the window's wreckage and stalked forward. Red light emanated from its obsidian eyes, displaying a deep cunning yet little malice, which was strange. The creature clearly intended to kill her if it could, yet she sensed an odd reluctance within it.

Still, dying one way was as good as another. So she ducked and then darted to one side, anticipating the stone creature's next move. But instead of swinging its cudgel, the stone behemoth struck the roof shingles. A main beam collapsed and if it were not for Mithla's heightened senses, she would have fallen through the gap to await her next incarnation.

She sidestepped the creature's next swing. Shattered tiles sprayed the air like lethal knives. Mithla leapt to the dome's railing and with a quick somersault landed on a support beam. Her assailant surged forward, battering aside Mithla's legendary sword.

With unerring precision, the shadow princess parried, then lunged for the creature's supposed eyes. Her sword thrummed and buckled, but had its desired effect. The creature gave a gravelly roar, then scrambled on to the dome's edge. Another flick of Mithla's sword and she prodded the creature's other red-lit cavity.

It floundered for a moment, its cudgel raised high as though to smash through the dome's frame. Mithla didn't wait for her opponent's next move. She flipped through the air, landed on the dome's rim behind the creature and pushed with all her might.

The creature toppled forward like a felled tree. Splintering the dome's framework as though it were kindling, the stone being fell five floors and shattered into fist-sized rocks on the library's tiled floor. Its many parts sprayed across the foyer like thrown marbles.

'There's one of them,' cried a voice.

'Fire!' came a command.

Mithla glided across the shingles. Crossbow bolts clicked and clattered against the brickwork. Several zinged by, one even catching her billowing cloak.

Mithla left the hubbub way behind. Within scant seconds she had led her pursuers a merry chase across several rooftops and down many darkened laneways. Satisfied that she had eluded the watch-men, she doubled back to the library's majestic dome. Scaling a rusting drainpipe, she climbed back through the window and slid down the pole, dropping nimbly to the carpeted balcony.

A faint light touched the horizon, and with it Mithla knew she must withdraw from Tamaika's body. Picking her way across the rock-dotted floor, she pulled the cellar door behind her and lay in a comfortable position in a leather-bound chair.

Cador to the Rescue

TAMAIKA WOKE WITH A start. Filtered light from the barred windows made her blink. She got to her feet, breathing heavily. Muffled voices drifted down from the stairwell from the main hall of the library above.

'You can search all you like, Sergeant, but I am telling you no one broke in here. There is no sign of entry apart from the dome in the Reading Room and our ward spells are quite intact.'

Head Librarian Tomes's voice went on monotonously. Other voices broke into excited chatter. Someone ordered everyone back to work and the voices quietened to whispers.

Tamaika took a step and almost fell. She looked down, but she hadn't tripped over anything. Her face ashen, she patted herself all over. What is happening to me? she wondered. Her book lay discarded on the floor, its spine almost broken. Dazed, she turned a full 360 degrees, taking deep breaths as she did so. Nothing had changed. She must have fallen asleep and dropped her book.

Thinking hard, she remembered picking up the *Princess of Shadows* and being consumed by … what? Consumed by magic? Brushing the thought aside she picked up *Rift Enchantress* and closed it. She would have to celebrate its publication another time.

Hiding the book beneath a pile of deeds and death certificates, Tamaika crept up the stairs. She couldn't afford to be caught in the cellar. She would be in enough trouble from her sisters already for not having gone home the night before. If only she could really be like the heroine in her dream.

She had barely unlatched the door when Hetta pulled it right open. 'She's here! Hiding, as usual,' she said. 'Found the little tramp,' she called to Byra and Gabra.

Tamaika fell straight into her woebegone persona, but not before noticing that her three sisters each clutched a hand mirror. Hetta actually had rouge smeared across her cheeks. More curiously, Byra's usually lank hair was tied into a bun. Tamaika's mouth dropped. Gabra's bloated lips had been painted plum red.

'What are you staring at?' Byra demanded. 'The chief constable isn't coming to speak to you, so get back down to the dungeon where you belong.'

With that, Hetta shoved Tamaika in the chest and pulled the door shut. Tamaika heard the ominous sound of a lock turning. Something welled up inside her and her hands clenched into fists. Before she knew what she was doing, she thumped on the door. The resultant sound reverberated throughout the foyer.

Tamaika had hit the door three times before she had the willpower to stop. Whatever possessed you to do that? she thought with alarm. You're in for it now. They'll flay you alive!

Predictably, Byra's scathing voice hissed, 'Bang on the door one more time, missy, and we'll hand you over to the dung brigade as an orphan. Now get back downstairs and not a word. Not a sound, you little turd.'

Tamaika forced her hands to unclench. She so wanted to smash the door down. Confused and breathless, she fled down the stairs. What had come over her? All the wheedling and despair that she could muster would never undo what she had just done. To openly defy her sisters was … unspeakable.

Pinpointed by a solitary shaft of light, Tamaika sat in her chair to await her release.

It was not long in coming. A key jangled in the lock and Tamaika stood quickly. Her chair fell back with a loud crash.

A uniformed man hurried down the stairs, his sword drawn. When he spotted Tamaika he said, 'Who's this then?'

With a start Tamaika realised it was the senior constable who had bought her book. Her heart hammered and she instantly coloured, thinking he must surely hear it. He looked as though he had stepped right out of a Brice Daggersure rift novel.

'Tamaika?' Head Librarian Tomes queried. 'What's the meaning of this? Have you been in here all night?'

With sudden inspiration, she whispered, 'I was locked in, Head Tomes.' She averted her eyes in case they betrayed her white lie.

'Let me,' the man said to Head Librarian Tomes. He sheathed his sword. 'I'm Chief Constable Cador,' he said gently. He looked back up the stairs. 'Did you hear a noise up there last night?'

Tamaika looked from Cador to Head Librarian Tomes, then back again. She nodded miserably.

'Why were you down here after closing?' demanded Head Librarian Tomes.

'Please, Miss Tomes,' Cador said. 'As just witnessed, the door was locked. You unlocked it yourself.'

'There are no signs of forced entry into the library, which means ...' Head Librarian Tomes began her litany.

Cador held up his hand for silence. 'My sergeant gave me your statement.' He looked back down at the quivering girl. He had recognised her immediately of course. She had a certain fragility, yet something else, too, which he had seen in the marketplace the day before. It showed in the way she stood. Defiant, yet deferential. Most peculiar for one of her station. It was the sort of chameleon characteristic he would expect from a master thief. He put his arm around her shoulder and led her up the stairs, past Head Librarian Tomes. 'I need to speak to her in private. She's obviously in shock. Whatever caused the mess in your library must have terrified her.'

Head Librarian Tomes nodded curtly. 'You know

where my office is, Chief Constable. Try not to keep her overlong.'

'As you wish, Head Librarian,' Cador said.

Byra, Gabra and Hetta fluttered around the doorway like butterflies.

'Refreshments, Chief Constable?' warbled Byra.

'Corn cups?' queried Gabra, flourishing a plate of cakes.

'Let me open the door for you, Chief Constable,' Hetta said, not to be left out.

'That will be all, ladies,' Cador said, closing the door on their overwrought painted faces.

'Well, Tamaika,' he said. 'You've had a most hectic day and night by all accounts. Perhaps you would care to share some of the highlights?'

Tamaika shrugged. 'I fell asleep downstairs. I was reading.'

'The inestimable Dacy Dunnard, I gather?'

Tamaika nodded forlornly.

Cador watched silently through a window as Tamaika's sisters sprinkled water across the marble floor and swept the spray of rocks from the foyer into a cairn in the atrium.

Tamaika saw them whirling like dervishes, each trying to outdo the other. Mainly, though, she noticed her sisters looking over at the office. She couldn't be sure, but each of them was batting her eyelashes as though dust was in her eyes.

'I haven't finished reading my copy,' Cador said, breaking the silence. 'And you?'

'It's good,' Tamaika said. Then quickly, 'I haven't finished it either, but what I've read is good. Dunnard's no Brice Daggersure, but …'

'Yet you fell asleep reading it?' Cador queried, still not facing her.

'I'd been reading and cataloguing all day in the cellar,' Tamaika explained. 'It's the ill light that wearies the eyes.'

Cador turned and smiled. 'You'd need to have goblin eyes to work down there for too long,' he commiserated. He deliberately boggled his eyes at her and she laughed. Then his smile dropped and he said, 'Have you any idea what caused the mess out there? Do you think a vandal sneaked in?'

'I have no idea,' Tamaika said, remembering the nightmare: a ghoulish stone creature that had tried to kill her. Or had that been real? She made an impatient gesture with her hand which Cador noted with interest. It's all getting mixed up now, thought Tamaika. Reality, dream … maybe she was going crazy like those poor souls up in the asylum who lived inside their bizarre fantasies, unable to tell the difference. The thought made her shudder and Cador noted this too. Tamaika knew one thing. Whatever had happened to her — or hadn't happened! — it was connected to the book, *Princess of Shadows*.

Hardly trusting herself to speak, she added, 'Head Tomes said there was no forced entry. Didn't she?'

Cador nodded, still watching her. 'Several times. But it's strange that my constables found a pole still attached to a dome window. Logic suggests that whoever caused the damage must have had inside help. The accomplice either left the pole attached to assist the vandal, or the vandal was already inside the library.'

Tamaika's mind spun with the implications. 'Your logic seems faultless,' she said slowly. 'However, it is possible that the ... vandal opened the window and left the pole attached while the library was open. It's my job to lock the windows and bar the doors.'

'And of course you were locked in the cellar and even fell asleep down there. So the open window with its pole attached went unnoticed,' Cador finished for her.

'That would be my guess,' Tamaika said, 'but I am no puzzle solver.'

'If only Dacy Dunnard were here,' Cador said, laughing. 'His plotting skills are such that I have no doubt he would puzzle out this problem in the blink of an eye.'

'You really think so?'

'I do.'

This was heady praise for Tamaika and it was on the tip of her tongue to blurt out the truth, but at the last second she backed away from it. 'I would beg a favour,' she said.

Cador waved her on.

'I will be reprimanded quite severely for my negligence regarding the dome windows. I would be eternally grateful if you would omit my negligence from your report.' What are you doing making demands of the chief constable? she thought wonderingly.

'I can't see how you could fulfil your duties when you were locked in the cellar,' Cador said. 'However, consider it done, young Tamaika. We fellow Dunnard readers must stick together. We're few enough as it is, this early in his career.'

'Her,' Tamaika said automatically. 'Dacy's a woman.'

'The devil you say!' Cador said.

The door opened and Head Librarian Tomes put her head into the room. 'Are you done, Chief Constable?'

'I think so,' Cador said. 'You have a very brave staff member here, Head Tomes. Any lesser person might have died from shock at what she saw through the keyhole.' He winked at Tamaika before facing the head librarian. 'Due to the very nature of this business I've forbidden her to discuss the episode with anyone. Is that understood?'

Head Librarian Tomes's mouth twitched. 'Completely.'

'You're lucky to have a library to open this morning, by all accounts,' Cador said as he left the room. 'Very lucky indeed. I believe it might have been Tamaika's frantic banging on the door that scared the vandals off.'

'Plural?' Head Librarian Tomes queried.

'Oh, there was more than one perpetrator here,' Cador confirmed.

Byra, Gabra and Hetta scurried over the moment

the chief constable left. 'Well,' Byra said, 'what have you got to say for yourself?'

'You're in for a flaying when you get home,' Hetta put in. 'Staying out all night. You'll get us girls a bad reputation, you will.'

Head Librarian Tomes raised her eyebrow at that. 'Tamaika will be saying nothing of her stay in the library last night. Is that understood, ladies?'

The three sisters simmered for a long moment. Then Byra said, 'We were just teasing her, Head Tomes. Come on then, Tamaika, we've cleaned up the worst of it. Workmen have begun repairing the dome. Begging your leave, Head, but I've assigned Tamaika to splash some water over the glass. It'll need proper cleaning as it's repaired.' She indicated a bucket of steaming water with several short-handled mops in it.

'Away you go, Tamaika,' Head Librarian Tomes said. 'And be careful. All things considered, it's a wonder the entire dome didn't fall in on us.'

Tamaika squeezed past her sisters, glad to be away. Byra could not have thought of a better punishment for her. She had been dying to get back on the roof to make sense of her nightmare.

She climbed the rungs to the roof, spilling as little

of the water as possible. Naturally, Byra had filled the bucket to the brim and had watched her like a hawk as she made for the fifth floor. She hadn't spilt a drop till she climbed the ladder.

Tamaika almost shrank back through the door when she saw Chief Constable Cador there, but he had already spotted her.

'Nasty business,' he called. He was currently inspecting a corner stone, where a squatting Hakogna had once sat hunched over, a silent sentinel looking across the Quentaran rooftops.

Tamaika went to him and looked down into the street. 'Did someone tip Figrid over?'

'Figrid?' Cador said, puzzled for a split second. 'Oh, I see. Figrid the Hakogna. No, I'd say the last of what's left of poor Figrid is being swept up as we speak.' He looked back at the workmen hammering a new brace across a shattered crossbeam. 'It's my guess that several people were involved here. Too heavy for one man to handle. They somehow prised Figrid from his perch, carried him to the dome, and threw him through the glass.'

'What a stupid thing to do. Someone could have been hurt,' Tamaika said quickly. Again, Cador's presence confused her. She tried to steer her thoughts elsewhere. Why would someone destroy Figrid? A prank? Or something more sinister? She sighed. Her confusion over Cador seemed to mix in with her confusion over last night. Was it really just a bad dream? Or was it a memory?

A question just seemed to jump out of her mouth. 'What if Figrid somehow came to life and attacked … the library?' Utterly preposterous, of course. She felt stupid even as she asked it. But Cador didn't laugh. Instead he looked at her queerly.

'What makes you say that?' he asked.

Emboldened, she said, 'A strange dream I had.' Then she laughed at herself, breaking the spell. 'Maybe I've been reading too much Dacy Dunnard.' But a thought came unbidden to her: her assailant could well have been the stone gargoyle come to life. 'I expect it's just the work of vandals.'

'That would be a pity. Vandals are seldom caught unless one has cultivated street informers and I am rather new to my post. Then again, vandalism usually reflects anger and dissatisfaction, and is the work of gangs, not individuals. It is not easy to get convictions. Nor would it explain why citizens are being turned to stone.'

'Stone?' She stared at him wide-eyed.

'We have tried to keep it a secret but I fear it will not be long before the truth is known. I do not wish for a panic.'

'I won't tell anyone.'

'I'm sure you won't. In any case, for now I must pursue the possibility that this was indeed the work of malcontents. We shall see.' He took a deep breath. 'According to Head Tomes there have been a few disgruntled patrons of late. The usual crackpots, complaining about this book and that, some not being worthy of inclusion in the collection. Missing pages, "censored" by self-appointed critics. Fined patrons refusing to pay for overdue books and the like. A dangerous and desperate crowd, I dare say.'

He was laughing at her, but she joined in. 'It's true. Certainly if looks could kill, few librarians would be now still breathing.'

Their laughter subsided. 'Seriously, though,' said Cador, 'no one person would be strong enough to carry Figrid ten yards and throw him through the dome. Clearly there were many hands at work here.'

'Or dark magic.'

Cador looked at her. 'So many questions and it's barely the eighth hour. I'd best depart.'

His eyes suddenly looked past her. 'Better fetch your bucket, Tamaika. One of the workers is cleaning his tools in it.'

The day progressed with monotonous predictability. Tamaika scrubbed, washed and rinsed the giant dome's two thousand and twenty-five glass panes to within an inch of their life, yet Byra still pointed out spots that she had missed. Three times she climbed the roof ladder with piping hot water; three times she reported back to Byra only to be told she was a lazy good-for-nothing. It became so dark in the end that not even Byra's eagle eyes could spot faults in Tamaika's workmanship. As the sun went down, the dome shone with a brilliance not seen since its installation. Then Head Librarian Tomes forbade Tamaika to work in the dark.

'Well, off home with you then,' Byra said magnanimously. 'And don't expect last night's chores to have been done for you. There's a kitchen full of dishes and whatnot. And we'll have supper at half past the eighteenth hour, your ladyship.'

'Thank you, Byra,' Tamaika said. She hurried

home as best she could through the darkened streets. Perhaps it was the excitement of it all, what with the previous night's events, meeting the chief constable, and even having her book published, but Tamaika felt quite invigorated when she arrived home. The prospect of cleaning a house left filthy by her three sisters and having to cook them supper had surprisingly little effect on her.

Coming in the door she heard the sound of dishes rattling in the kitchen.

'Papa?' Tamaika came up behind her father. He didn't turn around. 'You shouldn't be doing the dishes after a hard day's work at the docks. I'll make you some tea.'

Elad Erskona said nothing. He turned and walked past Tamaika, not glancing at her even once. His eyes seemed somewhat glazed and there was a profound sadness etched in the deep lines of his face.

'I was locked in the library all night,' Tamaika said, blinking back tears. 'I hope you weren't worried. I was perfectly safe.' Her father went into the living room and sat down, picking up a book. Tamaika boiled water and brewed a pot of spiced rift tea, his favourite. She put out a cup and a saucer, sugar, and some pastries.

She carried it in on a silver tray and placed it next to him then busied herself lighting a fire. Her father never spoke a word.

For a while she sat and watched him as he slowly read the book that he had read a thousand times. Her father hadn't spoken to her since their mother had died three years ago. The joy of life had left him that bleak winter afternoon when Cidra had breathed her last wheezing breath, despite all the potions and medicines they could buy. Tamaika had blamed herself for her mother's death. She had been out with her mother and had begged to go skating on the frozen river, despite her mother's protests. The ice had given way and Cidra had pushed Tamaika to safety and plunged into the frozen depths of the river. Beneath the ice the current was still strong and she was dragged underwater. By sheer luck some fishermen had cut a hole farther downstream and she popped up in this gap, already blue and unconscious. Quick thinking and the spell of a passing wizard had revived her, but she had never been the same. Three months later she had died.

Her father talked to Tamaika's sisters, though even then he rarely spoke in anything larger than monosyllables, a kind of verbal shorthand that all the sisters got to know.

But he never addressed anything to Tamaika, nor ever looked at her. The pain of that excommunication had been so enormous, his grief so inconsolable, that she had wanted to die herself.

'You must be famished,' she said, jumping up and pumping some water into a pot. 'I'll make us a wholesome turnip and vegetable soup. That will warm you up.'

Resigned that she would get nothing further from her father, Tamaika hid her face. She did not want him to see the pain there.

Tamaika rushed about the kitchen to be finished before her sisters arrived. The last thing she needed tonight was more of their bullying.

Cador Gets Help

THERE WERE MORE ATTACKS during the night. Corporal Serensen stood atop the north-west watchtower, gazing out across the rooftops and spires of night-enshrouded Quentaris. There was a little traffic in the streets below and yellow lamplight flickered behind curtained windows, but for the most part the streets were empty and the houses shuttered tight. Fear gripped the city. Serensen could feel it.

'Pack of old ladies,' he sneered quietly to himself. He had patrolled the watches and roofs of this city for more than fifteen years and never in all that time had he seen anything to put the wind up him. Oh, there were shadows right enough and odd goings-on (mostly youngsters he reckoned). There was danger too, that he had to admit. Sky pirates sometimes drifted out of the rift caves, floating on great sky-ships, to raid and plunder the city. Not to mention the Zolka! Oh, there'd been some hot times, that was sure enough.

But this latest malarky! People turned to stone! What rot. Somebody had had a bit too much to drink, he thought, wishing for a drop of Old Dragonish himself. There was a cruel, cold wind blowing down from the rift caves and he rubbed his hands vainly to put back some warmth back into them. Then he heard a sound that made his blood run cold.

He half-turned; saw the slab of rough-hewn darkness reaching for him, piercing eyes glowering. And he screamed.

The scream ended abruptly. With a sound like crunching glass, he turned instantly to stone. Out across the city other watchmen jolted awake and stared in the direction of the north-east watchtower, shivering at the dead echo of that scream.

Chief Constable Cador was tired. He had been up most of the night dealing with the latest rampage: mindless destruction of public property and wide-spread looting — though he strongly suspected this had more to do with the impoverished rapscallion roofies than with the attackers. Twenty-eight citizens had also been turned to stone, most of them high-ranking, important people, the kind with indignant and powerful relatives.

He flinched, remembering the tongue-lashing he had received from the father of a wealthy banker who had been transmogrified while sitting on his toilet. Added to the indignity of such a circumstance — scandalous in its own right, as if the rich and powerful did not need to excrete like the lower orders — the man had been related distantly to the Nibhellines. No doubt there would be further political repercussions. His head ached at the mere thought.

After ensuring that the attacks had indeed ended, Cador interviewed two witnesses. The watchmen swore they saw gigantic twenty-foot winged trolls leaping from building to building. After tripling the Watch for the night and ordering huge bonfires lit in all the squares, Cador finally returned home and climbed wearily into bed, desperate for sleep.

But sleep did not come.

Instead, his head buzzed with odd facts and figures: twenty-eight new 'statues', two possible witnesses, one watchman lost, sixteen houses broken into, five nights in a row, a thousand years since the Hakogna had supposedly arisen … less than four months in the job as acting chief constable.

He picked up *Rift Enchantress* in desperation; hoping that it would distract him, maybe even send him to sleep. Several hours later he reluctantly closed the book on a marker and placed it gently on his bedside table. *Enchantress* had been written by a deft hand. An extraordinary first novel, full of the exact kind of romance and adventure in the rift caves that he had once longed for himself, before family duty dashed all such adolescent hopes.

As much as he had enjoyed the book, he had also studied each page for clues as to what was threatening Quentaris. Seers like Godrund might speak in symbols and riddles at times, but they invariably spoke truth — if the listener could but interpret it. In this regard, Cador had failed miserably, but he made a note to himself that he needed to meet this Dacy Dunnard. Perhaps the author, knowing her own work in ways others could not, would be able to shed light on the puzzle.

But he didn't have time to dwell on it now. He had a meeting with the Archon, Lord Chalm Eftangeny, in exactly one hour. And before that ordeal he definitely needed a shave and a hearty breakfast, not to mention something to remove the bags from under his eyes.

At the appointed time he was shown into the Mahogany Room by Manasseh, Lord Chalm's chamberlain. Cador took a seat at what the Archon liked to call the war table. Commander Storm was there, as was a rift wall sergeant called Red and the Archon himself.

Lord Chalm rapped the table for attention. Satisfied he had it, he said, 'Commander Storm, what have you to report?'

'Not much, I'm afraid, my lord. As you know, most of my people have been seconded to wall duty. The Zolka have been swarming of late. I've had every available watchman on alert from the first to the last hour since this business began, but apart from brief sightings and the usual rumours, we're no closer to identifying the culprits.'

Chief Constable Cador winced inwardly. He was fully aware of what the commander was saying. Storm's casual reference to the Zolka was, if anything, an understatement. Guarding the caves was labour-intensive and often dangerous; the watchmen were critically short-staffed right now, which left the onus on Cador's investigative constabulary to sort out the mess.

The Archon looked sourly at both Cador and Storm. 'Sightings? Rumours?' he said. 'Is there nothing certain?' He leaned forward, fixing them both with a somewhat paranoid stare. 'Are my enemies rising against me?'

Commander Storm looked over at Cador. 'My guess, my lord, is that we have a rogue wizard on our hands. Not a local, I'd say, probably one from Tolrush. One who has an axe to grind. Someone we've most likely exiled in the past.'

The Archon sat back and grunted. 'I gather we've drawn up a list of such individuals? Sought their current whereabouts? Started interrogations?'

'It's not altogether as easy as that,' Commander Storm said uneasily. 'Exiled wizards can vanish into thin air, as the saying goes.'

'All right, all right,' Lord Chalm said impatiently. 'Look into it as best you can. My ablest spies are at your disposal. Sergeant Red, I gather we have no illegal immigrants? All rift adventurers have been thoroughly checked on entry from their sojourns?'

The red-bearded wall guard nodded. 'We've had few incidents of late. Shape-shifters and the like are always hard to detect. But to the best of my knowledge, nothing untoward has passed the rift wall.'

The Archon's eyes fell on the inexperienced Cador. 'And what have you to say, *Deputy* Chief Constable?' he asked.

Cador shuffled some papers. 'At first we thought it might be disgruntled goblins out for a bit of mischief. But we've dismissed that theory. I've visited both Nilus and Godrund. They were their mysterious selves, but did not seem overworried.'

'I should think not,' the Archon sniffed. 'Nothing's likely to happen to them personally, is it? I trust you are reporting to your father all the while. Great man, your father.'

Cador smiled awkwardly. 'Father's been most helpful,' he lied. How could he tell the Archon that his father had not opened his eyes or spoken in the past week? If he admitted that he was acting alone, Lord Chalm would replace him in an instant. And slowly perhaps, but just as surely, House Mercutis would slide into ruin.

'What else do you have there, young Cador?' the Archon asked.

'Not much, my lord,' Cador admitted. 'One of the Hakogna was thrown through the Great Library Reading Room dome.'

'Relevance?' Lord Chalm interrupted.

'Tenuous,' Cador admitted. 'But I've been looking into the Hakogna history. The original horde attacked Quentaris two thousand years ago and was repelled by a magician army. As penance for their invasion, the remainder of them were turned to stone and forced to watch after the city's safety for eternity. It appears that in times of great peril, they must animate and set things right. Simple-minded myth of course, since there is no substantiating evidence, but this "myth" is chronicled in some detail in *The Compleat Book of Mythology and Magic*.'

Lord Chalm looked unimpressed. 'So we're resorting to fairy tales now, are we?' he grumbled. 'They're stone gargoyles, Chief Constable. Sculpted by master tradesmen from a bygone era. You really do need to consult your father on these matters. And perhaps you should talk to your brother. Smart lad, that Maxon. But as for fairy tales? Load of rubbish. There's flesh and blood behind this, Cador, flesh and blood! Or my name's not Lord Chalm.'

Neither Commander Storm nor Sergeant Red

commented. Closeted away in his castle, Lord
Chalm had never had to deal with the more evil, and
magical, denizens that often rampaged through
Quentaris. Death and mayhem on parchment, or
even in second-hand reportage, never did quite
reveal its true horror.

Lord Chalm looked over at his scribe, ignoring
Cador's discomfort. 'All done then, got all that?'

The scribe nodded.

'Very well,' the Archon concluded. 'I suppose it is
a little early to be expecting results. But I want this
mess cleaned up. I can't have our city's most influential citizens being turned to rock like a bunch of
garden gnomes.' He shuddered then, recalling how
some of the victims had been scrunched up into a
foetal position before being turned into stone, their
faces in a grimace of terror. 'By the way, Chief
Constable, where are you storing them? Out of
harm's way I hope. I can't begin to imagine what the
peasants will be doing to them while they're defenceless.'

No more than what's been done to them all their
lives, Cador thought. He said, 'I've placed them
under heavy guard in a warehouse, my lord.'

'Well and good,' Lord Chalm said. 'And I want

our best people on this case.' He stopped at a sudden thought. 'The magic *is* reversible, is it not? We can turn them back to flesh and blood again?'

'What's conjured can usually be unconjured, where wizardry is concerned,' Cador said. 'But during my talks with Nilus and Godrund, they implied we need to find what they called the "source magic". Only by locating that can anyone unravel it.'

'See to it,' the Archon said, closing the meeting.

'See to it,' Cador muttered as he inspected his men's positions on the rooftops of Quentaris that evening. 'Easier said than done.'

'You said something?' asked Maxon.

Cador turned to find his twin brother gazing at him. Maxon had uncharacteristically offered to help in the defence of the city. Cador had only accepted to appease the Archon. 'Just thinking aloud,' he said. 'I think I've covered every angle, don't you? I have my constables on every tall building in the city. There's hardly a square yard of shingle that isn't laid bare to my people. More to the point, the walls are now heavily guarded and I've requested the city's mages triple the watch and ward spells on our outer defences, as well as the approaches to Quentaris, especially on the north side facing the caves.'

They were currently standing at the base of the golden minaret atop the Cathedral of the Holy Benefactor Mushin. Night had fallen quickly and a cold wind blew down from the snow-covered mountains. Maxon pulled his cloak closer to him before answering. 'All very well, brother, yet if the evil is within, rather than without, then what good your carefully laid plans?'

Cador let the chill wind whip his face. 'And what would you advise, Maxon?'

Maxon spread his hands, shrugging. 'You're so defensive, brother. I am sure you have thought of everything. You are always so … thorough.'

Cador was about to ask his brother to elaborate, but warning bells began pealing and men and women raised their voices in hoarse shouts, which other voices picked up and echoed across the city. His sword rasped as it left its scabbard. 'It begins,' he said.

'I see nothing,' Maxon said, peering out across the silvery Quentaran skyline. He shivered but whether from fear or the sharp wind, Cador could not tell.

A snarling dark shape climbed suddenly over the

parapet into full view. Cador pulled his brother back and pushed past him to meet the creature head on. 'What manner of beast is this?' he said, his eyes wide and staring. Then his sword met his assailant's cudgel and the clamour of this and many other battles rose above the city.

Even as he fought, Cador had trouble believing what he was seeing. As steel grated against the stone cudgel and sparks stabbed the air, he realised that if he did not pay more attention to this fight he would never live to unravel the mystery. His assailant suddenly lunged, bringing the cudgel around in a blurring arc that would have torn Cador in two. He leapt back, deflected the strike with his sword, yet cried out as the impact shocked through his sword arm. He barely managed to parry the next blow, swiftly riposte, duck back and narrowly avoid an attacker who had come up behind him.

'Maxon?' Cador called, but his brother had already fled the walkway, abandoning him. How very like Maxon!

Two more of the creatures climbed over the parapet. Above them, clouds scudded away, bathing the rooftop in bright moonlight. Hakogna! his numbed mind told him. The gargoyles have come to life! But how?

Yet another stone creature hauled itself slowly over a crenellation. Cador avoided their attempt to corner him and backed away, scanning the entire base of the minaret, realising there was nowhere left to go. Now cornered, his back against the spire of the minaret itself, he could retreat no farther. With four of the enemy closing in on him, lethal cudgels raised high, he had little option but to make a rush for the parapet and — if he were lucky enough to break through the encircling Hakogna — leap to a lower balcony, itself a deadly drop of some twenty yards.

Cador tensed himself for the charge, then stopped and slowly straightened, chuckling softly to himself. If he were to meet his end this night, then he would do so fighting. He was not Maxon; he would not run away. Just then something landed on the minaret spire above him. Instinctively he swung his sword in a high defensive arc.

Tamaika felt not the least bit inclined to retire for the night, yet it was the only peace she could find in their small home. The attic space was cramped and cloying but she snuggled up on her straw pallet beside an oil lamp. Its guttering flame illuminated the rough draft of her next book. She carefully dipped her quill into the ink and began writing.

She had just finished the third page when her head began to spin. Thinking it was the light, she wound up the wick on the lamp, but her dizziness didn't abate. It swept through her like an unstoppable wave. She staggered off the pallet, desperate to call for help, but her throat constricted, stifling her cry. She collapsed to the floorboards, her breath clogged.

'What's going on up there?' one of her sisters called out.

Barely able to breathe, Tamaika almost passed out, and then life-giving air rushed back into her lungs as though she were breaking the surface of a pond after being on the brink of drowning. Dazed, she looked down at herself. She had turned into the swashbuckling, masked Mithla again.

'I'm fine,' she responded hoarsely. Even her voice had deepened.

Her sister's shadow touched the attic stairs. 'Well, keep it down or I'll come and give you what for!'

Watching the low hung rafters, Mithla stepped

back from the ladder. 'Something must have gone down the wrong way,' she said, feigning a cough.

Her sister moved away from the ladder and Mithla went swiftly to the roof window. Shortly, she was scaling a drainpipe. Her keen eyes spotted many people on the rooftops. Some of them were roofies, the roof-loving populace that vowed never to put their feet on the cobbled streets. Others she noted were probably thieves, going about their nightly trade. She spotted silent figures, too, keeping watch. But none of this interested her as much as the city's mythical guardians — the Hakogna.

She moved across the shingles with a cat's agility. Several people called out for her to stop, but she paid no heed to their demands. Panther-like, she swept across the skyline.

Alarm bells sounded. There was a riot of shouting. Mithla smiled behind her black mask. It had begun. With cat-like vision, she saw four Hakogna stir into life. They uncurled and stretched their stiff limbs, then like lumbering beasts they climbed the sheer façade of the Cathedral of the Holy Benefactor Mushin.

Mithla jogged back several steps until she had a good run up to the edge of the building. The cathedral was a thirty-yard span from where she stood.

With the wind behind her, she hoped that she could just make the jump. If not, she might land on one of the balconies that ringed the cathedral at various heights. Too late to save whoever was now being set upon by the Hakogna, of course. But she might at least avenge them.

She ran full pelt for the ledge and jumped. The chasm yawned below her. Two watchmen in the street below happened to be looking up at that moment. As Mithla sailed across the yawning gap between buildings, her cape billowing out behind her, the men's jaws dropped and they inscribed across their chests the sign to ward off evil. To them, Mithla looked like a vampire etched against the silvery moon.

Mithla landed on all fours, clinging to the smooth surface of the minaret spire.

Without a moment of respite, Mithla unsheathed her sword and slid down the golden spire. She deftly knocked aside Cador's sword as he brought it up in defence and dropped beside him. 'Take those two,' she ordered, leaping at the other two Hakogna with a ferocity that made them take a step backwards. One aimed a well-placed blow at her head and she took the full brunt of the cudgel's impact without flinching. Then with Herculean strength, she forced the stone creature back into the attack zone of his brethren, fouling all attempts to get at Mithla and Cador. The others soon swarmed back, but there was little room to manoeuvre and they, too, were straining to keep their ground.

Behind her Cador cried out in alarm and stumbled. 'The stairs — they're our only hope,' he said. The battle had taken them to the far side of the spire where the door was located. He reached for it, then for an insane moment froze. Their eyes met. 'It's locked,' he said in disbelief.

Mithla weighed up the situation then. 'Whatever you do, don't let them touch you.' Acting with the speed of thought, she sprang at the Hakogna and quickly cut a way through them, dragging Cador behind her. They skirted the minaret, but were soon trapped again.

'Get behind me,' Mithla yelled. Cador protested, but Mithla swept him back with her free arm. Cador felt the power of that gesture and wondered at this slip of a girl who stood now between him and these monsters.

Mithla backed into the corner which jutted out from the rooftop, being the top of a flanged tower. The way to this protruding corner was via a narrow

path called a 'waist'. Here the two groups of gargoyles, which had charged from either side of the
minaret, ground into one another.

But the topography of the rooftop would not save
them for long. Mithla suddenly raised her sword
high, point downwards, then drove the sword into
the rooftop, crying out in a guttural language that
Cador had never heard before, but which the
Hakogna clearly understood. They froze. A shock
wave shot out from the point of impact, rippling
through the rooftop, toppling the Hakogna. They
climbed back to their feet, wary now. Then, as a
bright light came from where the sword was embed-
ded in the roof, they took a step backwards. Then
another as the ethereal light intensified.

'Close your eyes,' Mithla ordered Cador. With a
ferocious gush the light suddenly blasted outwards in
all directions, buffeting the Hakogna brutally. One
was flung from the rooftop and sent crashing to the
street below. The rest, startled, fell back, grunting in
their gravelly voices.

Mithla yanked the sword from the roof, swaying
slightly. The drain on her was tremendous. 'That
might even things up a bit,' Mithla wheezed. She set
upon the blinded gargoyles, hacking at them as she

would a clinging jungle vine. Chips and sparks spat and splattered. Mithla pursued the gargoyles around the perimeter of the minaret. Sensing their impending destruction, the Hakogna blindly scampered over the crenellations and rumbled away down the cathedral's walls.

Panting, Mithla watched them go for a moment, considering whether she had the energy to pursue them. She judged by their erratic retreat that they would be blinded for several hours yet. And there was much peril elsewhere this night.

She swung around when she heard a banging on the door. Cador opened it hesitantly.

Maxon appeared, pale and shaken. 'You're alive,' he said to Cador. He looked back at the door. 'It was locked. I pulled and pulled, but it remained stuck.'

Maxon saw Mithla and stopped. Then he brushed past his brother. 'Who are you?' he demanded.

'We owe her our lives,' said Cador.

Mithla bowed slightly. 'There is no debt, save one older than you can know, in whose service I am bound,' she said, then without any further ado she leapt over the parapet.

'No!' Cador cried, rushing toward her. He looked

down, expecting to see the woman's body broken upon the courtyard flags. But there was no sign of her. Only vaguely did he hear a sound like something flapping in the wind.

Maxon joined him. 'A rift vampire I'll warrant,' he said, 'but such a wondrous creature I have not seen.' He stopped, as though coming to his senses. 'You're lucky to have escaped with your life.'

Cador eyed his twin. 'Indeed I am. And the night is still young.'

With that, he hurried down the stairs to the sound of more alarm bells. Maxon followed anxiously behind.

7

The Stone Father

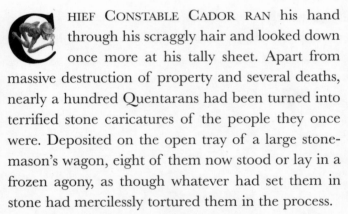

HIEF CONSTABLE CADOR RAN his hand through his scraggly hair and looked down once more at his tally sheet. Apart from massive destruction of property and several deaths, nearly a hundred Quentarans had been turned into terrified stone caricatures of the people they once were. Deposited on the open tray of a large stone-mason's wagon, eight of them now stood or lay in a frozen agony, as though whatever had set them in stone had mercilessly tortured them in the process.

Three constables covered the 'statues' with tarpaulins, then motioned the wagon driver to be on his way. The wagon started off with a creak, groaning under the weight. Cador's deputy, a lean man of forty years, came and stood beside Cador. 'Well, the way the town's old gargoyles are being taken down and carted away, we'll soon have enough lifelike replacements,' he joked.

'Not for a moment do I take this in humour, G'ladd,' Cador said. 'I'd be pleased for you to remember that.'

The deputy clenched his teeth and nodded sourly.

'How goes the demolition?'

G'ladd shrugged uncomfortably. 'I've been meaning to talk to you about that, chief.'

'A problem?'

'Aye, you might say that.' G'ladd spat on the ground, as if he didn't like the taste in his mouth. 'We've been demolishing the cursed things as fast as we could haul 'em down off the rooftops. But quick as we do it, they're even quicker at puttin' themselves back together.'

Cador stared. 'What's that?'

'Like I said. We bust 'em up, they mend themselves. Whatever's holding 'em together, it's powerful binding magic.'

'Have you tried scattering their remains?'

'Aye, we did that. Slowed 'em down a tad, but that's all. We dumped two in the river, scattered all over like. But what's the betting that come nightfall they will wade up outta the bay, none the worse for the inconvenience?'

Cador expelled a heavy sigh. 'I'm not one of those who would take that bet.'

'Me neither,' said G'ladd, gloomily.

'Has this city ever seen an evil like this?' Cador murmured, more to himself than G'ladd. To the latter he said, 'Cancel all leave, G'ladd. The Archon has declared martial law from this night on. And we're to be on round-the-clock alert. I fear we'll not rest again till we've rid our fair city of this scourge.'

Before G'ladd could reply, someone called out to the chief constable. 'Chief, there's a Tamaika Erskona here to see you.' Cador motioned to the man to let her through. When he saw the bruising on both her face and arms his eyes widened. 'What happened to you, Tamaika?'

The obviously distraught girl slumped when she reached him. 'It's Papa,' she said. 'Last night, he … oh, Cador, he is one of those who has been turned to stone!'

And she collapsed in his arms, sobbing.

After visiting the warehouse so Tamaika could see that her father's statue was being taken care of, Cador dropped Tamaika off at her house. Her sisters were standing on the door stoop awaiting her return. Sensing trouble, Cador escorted her to the door.

'All her fault!' Byra said.

'How could you?' Gabra seethed.

'Nothing but a tramp, staying out all night like that,' Hetta sniffed. 'Again.'

'Now what's all this about?' Cador asked.

'I'd have thought Tamaika would have confessed to you, Chief Constable,' Byra said, the tone of her voice softening to that of a cheese-grater on wood. 'She went out last night and our dear father, worried sick he was, went looking for her. Only he didn't return. Did he, Tamaika?'

Tamaika stared at Byra. Her hand groped out and found Cador's, clutching it for support. 'Papa was worried about me?' she asked, her voice like that of a small girl's. 'He went looking for me? For *me*?'

'Exactly,' said Byra. 'Who could imagine? We tried to stop him. Told him you weren't worth the effort. But no, off he went, fixated like some berserker.'

Tamaika felt like she might faint. 'He went looking for me,' she said again, almost to herself.

Cador gestured the three spiteful sisters aside and guided Tamaika through the door. 'Are you ladies not working this day?' he asked.

'We're only waiting so long, so hurry up, Tamaika,' Gabra said, munching on a haunch of bacon. 'You'll make us all late, what with your tardiness.'

Cador held up his hand. 'Tamaika won't be joining you today. She's been through a lot and needs to rest. Please relay her apologies to Head Tomes. If there's a problem, mention my name.' Before the sisters could say a thing, he pulled the door shut.

Sitting Tamaika down on a kitchen chair, he said, 'If it's any consolation, Tamaika, I'm also out of my depth.' He dropped into a chair beside her, exhausted. 'And just as your father lies entombed in stone, so mine lies entombed in a coma from which he may never awaken.'

Tamaika stared at Cador. Her thoughts were miles away. She felt an odd kind of joy and it took a moment for Cador's words to register. 'Oh, I'm sorry. You must be very sad.'

'You're the one I'm concerned about,' he said gently. 'But I fear we are as helpless as each other in the face of these things.'

'But you're the chief constable. You always know what to do.'

'If only that were true,' Cador said. 'Against the wishes of the Archon, shopkeepers are boarding up their shops before first dark; schools are closing; and rift travel has come to a near standstill as word has spread that Quentaris is in the grip of some bizarre rift plague.' He paused to rub his face, as if that might re-energise him. 'The Nibhellines and Duelphs are each blaming one another for the catastrophe. Worse, no one knows how the invaders are entering the city since the gates and walls have not been breached and the sewers and storm drains are all guarded. Our magicians are failing us. Clearly, some kind of powerful magic is at work here.'

Tamaika tested her arm, wincing several times. It was unbelievably sore.

'How did you sustain such injuries?' he asked suddenly.

Tamaika met his steady gaze with her own. 'I was sleep walking,' she said, improvising. 'Before I knew it I was in the streets. People were running for their lives and rocks began to fall from the roofs. I … must have been hit, for the next thing I remember I had staggered back home to bed.'

Cador nodded, eyeing her. 'I've heard of the like,' he said, a slight puzzlement in his voice. 'Perhaps you need to tie yourself up of a night. It might save your life next time.'

He stood. 'I should get back to my men,' he said. 'And somehow I must try to get a couple of hours sleep, otherwise I shall be useless when night falls.'

He moved to the door. 'I think you need rest also. Do not worry about your father. We believe the spell can be reversed.'

'But you do not know for certain.'

He dropped his gaze slightly. 'No. We do not. But we hope.'

With that he turned and departed. Tamaika sat for a long time with her legs drawn up and her chin resting on her knee, thinking. The ghost of a smile played about her lips.

It was dark inside the warehouse and bitterly cold. No doubt the stone statues — former citizens of

Quentaris — had no complaint in that regard, but Tamaika shivered almost uncontrollably, clutching her robe more tightly to herself. She suspected her shivering was not entirely due to the freezing temperatures.

Her breath steaming, she made her way anxiously through the crowd of statues. She found her father on his knees, his face upturned, a grimace of disbelief etched there. It was as if he had seen something incomprehensible dropping out of the sky towards him.

'Hello, Papa,' she said. She approached cautiously, as if he still had the power to reject her, to cause her pain. She dropped her gaze for a moment, murmuring, 'I didn't mean for this to happen, Papa. Any of it.' She slowly lowered herself to her knees beside him. He did not look at her now any more than he had in life.

She knelt there a long time, saying nothing, as still and silent as her father.

'I always wanted you and Mama to be so proud of me. Do you remember when I was eight and I said I wanted to be a writer? That I would write novels when I grew up? Well, I have. Look.' She took a copy of *Rift Enchantress* from under her robe and showed it to her father. 'It's a bestseller. Can you imagine that? Everybody's reading it. Why, the publisher thinks he may have to do a second edition.'

Her voice had grown excited. Faint echoes of it rebounded inside the great warehouse. Tamaika swallowed, went to stand, but stopped.

'I need you so badly, Papa,' she said, and the sound of that little girl she had once been crept back into her voice. 'So much is happening. I'm turning into this — this ancient enchantress called Mithla and she has to save Quentaris from what's going on and I don't know how I feel about that. It's very scary but it's also kind of — well, it's kind of exciting, too. Like she gets to live the life I've always dreamed about. She's stronger than me, and she thinks really fast, and she's afraid of nothing. Imagine, Papa, being afraid of nothing in the whole world. I'd never imagined what that would be like. I feel like I've been scared my whole life. The only time I ever felt safe was when I was lost in some wonderful story or … when you used to hold me.'

Tears sprang into her eyes and she wiped at them irritably.

'I didn't mean for Mama to fall in the river that day,' she blurted suddenly, years of anguish gushing out with the words. 'I didn't mean for it to happen, Papa. I didn't, I didn't, please believe me.'

Tamaika buried her head against his cold stone chest and wept like a child. Her tears streamed down his granite shirt and puddled on the floor.

She cried for a long time, but finally lifted her head, sniffling and wiping her nose. She felt better, which was odd, considering that her father had not said a thing.

She placed the copy of *Rift Enchantress* in the crook of his arm. It fitted snugly there. She got to her feet and turned to go, then turned back.

'Do you believe in love at first sight, Papa?' Her voice was just a whisper. 'Is that how it was between you and Mama? Did you take one look at one another and just know that here was the person you wanted to grow old with?'

Her father stared back stonily but Tamaika smiled, wiping away the remainder of her tears.

'I think I have.'

She turned and left, her heart lighter than it had been in a long time.

'How are your investigations going?' Tamaika asked Cador the next day when he dropped in to see how she was. The city was full of talk of the Princess of Shadows. Somehow, the word had spread. People knew that Mithla had come back from the dead, but whether to help or hinder seemed unknown.

Cador leaned back in his chair, weary beyond belief. He had spent another night battling Hakogna and had run into Mithla for a second time. 'I'm baffled as to where this Princess of Shadows comes into it all.'

Tamaika's voice had an odd catch in it as she said, 'People are saying she's to blame.'

'People say a lot of things when they're scared, but I know such rumours to be false. Of course, the only way I can prove that with any certainty is to meet this legendary woman that some insist does not exist.' Tamaika went to speak, but thought better of it. Cador wondered what she might have said then went on. 'I've finished reading Dacy Dunnard's *Rift Enchantress*, by the way.'

'Did you enjoy it?' Tamaika asked quietly.

'Indeed I did. But what struck me most of all was that it reminded me of something. Dunnard's description of the enchantress fits perfectly with that of the Princess of Shadows. Her cloak and raiment are slightly different, but nonetheless, on close inspection …'

'Yes, I had noticed that,' Tamaika agreed. 'Do you think there is a connection?'

'Who knows? The similarity ends there,' Cador said. 'But *Rift Enchantress* is a powerful love story. It kept me awake when I should have been sleeping.' He scoffed at himself. 'It was as though our friend Dunnard had cast a spell upon the book to hook the reader from page one to the very end.'

A deep delight swelled within Tamaika that she tried hard to quell. 'Do you eagerly await the next book?'

'Indeed I do, if such an item is produced,' Cador said. 'More than anything I would love to meet the author. But according to the publisher, the manuscript was delivered by courier, with a note saying the royalties should be donated to the Orphans' Hospital.'

'We might never know who she is,' Tamaika said. She pushed away from the table and stood. 'I really must go to work. It will distract me from thought of my papa.'

'A busy mind is an occupied mind,' Cador said.

'And fear not for your father. He is probably safer than most of us right now.' He went with her to the door. 'I'll bid you farewell, Tamaika. And rest assured, I will not rest until I have ended this plague on Quentaris.'

'I believe you,' Tamaika said, and left for work. Despite the fact that she just knew she would be cleaning out inkwells all day for her insolence, not even that could dampen the pleasure in her heart. Cador loved her book! He thought she was a real writer. This learned and respected man admired her authorship. Now if only her father were returned to them, her heart would know no end of joy.

Cador watched Tamaika till she was lost from view. He shook his head fondly and returned to his office. Maxon looked up from a book in his hands when the door opened. He tossed the tome on the desk.

'I thought you read literature, brother mine,' Maxon said. 'Not trash.'

'Perhaps you would care to define the word "literature", Maxon?' Cador said, carefully picking up *Rift Enchantress*. 'The woman who wrote this I daresay could write for the city's *Great Chronicles*, such is her passion and mastery of the written word.' He smiled despite the proximity of his shiftless brother. 'In fact, I'd go so far as to admit that I could easily fall in love with such a mind.'

Maxon heaved a sigh. 'You're a foolish dreamer, Cador. What good are tales of fiction and their dubious authors? Life is to be lived, not written down and pored over by those who have no lives.'

'And for such a belief you shall be bound to mediocrity,' Cador said. 'Now, I gather you're here on official business?'

8

Quentaris in Chaos

THE FOLLOWING WEEK SAW Quentaris totter into utter chaos. In complete panic, Lord Chalm decreed that the rifts closed to all traffic. A city of tents had sprung up on the no-man's-land between the wall and the rift caves, for re-entry into Quentaris had been banned until further notice.

Curfews and armed squads patrolling day and night were to no avail. The homes of the influential were broken into, their inhabitants turned to stone in their sleep.

Cador let the pile of reports drop to his desk. It had not gone unnoticed that it was mostly his brother's political enemies who had felt the brunt of the recent attacks. It was the sort of 'luck' that Maxon had always enjoyed. If he had dropped a silver moon down a drain, he would somehow discover a gold royal in the gutter beside the grate.

Despite his best efforts, Cador had come no closer to meeting the costumed woman whom some were now blaming for their woes again. It also appeared that only he and Maxon had seen the Hakogna come to life and survived to tell the tale. He suspected others had seen them, but were too afraid to come forward for fear of ridicule. Maxon refused to admit to the sightings, since it would mean political ruin. Maxon did, however, seem consumed with finding the costumed woman, who he fervently believed was Mithla.

Cador snorted. At least his brother's obsession would keep him occupied. Personally, he could almost believe his costumed saviour was nothing but a figment of his imagination. He shook his head. Most of the buildings around Quentaris had been stripped of their gargoyles, not that they stayed down for long, but the fact that the raids had continued unabated made Cador's Hakogna theory seem groundless.

On sudden inspiration, Cador began writing a brief message. He called out to G'ladd.

'Yes, sir?' the deputy said.

Cador folded the parchment, sealed it with wax and passed it to him. 'G'ladd, I want you to deliver this missive to a Tamaika Erskona at the Great Library. Be snappy, man, I need to talk to her urgently.'

Byra watched the deputy hand deliver an official letter. Gabra and Hetta appeared like moths to light. They weighed Tamaika's shoulders down with their chins in their eagerness to see what the message said.

'Why would the chief constable need to see you?' Byra demanded. 'What have you been up to now?'

Tamaika's cheeks flushed.

'You can't go till you've finished cataloguing the civil reports,' Byra said smugly. Gabra and Hetta smiled malevolently.

Emboldened by the chief constable's attention, Tamaika squared her shoulders, neatly dislodging the chins of Gabra and Hetta. 'I suggest that if there's an urgency to have the reports catalogued, you do it yourself,' she said.

Speechless with rage, Byra spluttered something unintelligible as Tamaika swept out of the library.

She didn't make directly for the chief constable's building. Instead, she found herself taking a slight detour home. She quickly washed herself down with some rose water and changed into her one good outfit. She looked at herself in the mirror and ruffled the sleeves and pulled the cuffs up. On impulse she unclipped the tight collar. Before she knew it, she was unpinning her hair and stroking it briskly with a brush.

Satisfied with what she saw in the mirror, she made a minor adjustment to her fringe by pinning it back with a fairy clip, then hurried to her appointment.

Cador beckoned her into his office and offered her a chair. Taking one himself behind his overburdened desk, he said, 'Thank you for coming at such short notice. I hope I didn't interrupt anything important.'

'Not at all,' Tamaika said distantly. The chief constable was dressed in the princely uniform of House Mercutis. Shining epaulettes rode his shoulders and medals hung from his blazing red tunic. His britches were jet black with a yellow and red stripe stitched along the seams. Tamaika was somewhat overwhelmed.

Cador looked down at himself. 'Please excuse all this buffoonery. It's … required today. A ceremonial matter to do with my mother.'

Tamaika sat silently in awe. Somehow she managed to nod quickly, but she knew that a flush had spread across her cheeks.

'Right,' Cador said, sensing the girl's remoteness. 'I cannot help but think that somehow you are linked to this little dilemma we have.' He held up a hand. 'Please hear me out. I've no one else to speak to on this matter. My deputies are fluttering about the place like chickens without heads, the Archon has barricaded all but the city's skyline and quite frankly, I am at a loss as to how I might proceed.'

Tamaika shifted uncomfortably.

'It's almost too inconceivable to be true, but it's my theory that the Hakogna are being roused from their slumber to perform the will of some iniquitous magician.' He laughed nervously. 'We both know the folk tale and I suspect you're more than aware that many horrors escape the rifts — but for our ward spells, Quentaris would have been overrun centuries ago.'

'I have heard rumours,' Tamaika admitted. 'Many of the invasions are kept from the public to avoid mass panic. So I have heard.'

Cador nodded sombrely. 'For one such as myself

to voice publicly such an admission would mean jail and loss of my title,' he said. 'I've gone out on a limb and against much public pressure taken down most of the Hakogna. People are saying that I'm a raving lunatic.' He thought for a second. 'Nothing and no one has been allowed into the city since Leshday, and yet the carnage continues unabated. The enemy is within. Obviously in the case of the Hakogna, a magic of the most powerful kind imaginable would need to be invoked to control them. Or else some nameless evil has slept for an eternity and has awakened.'

'Maybe the Hakogna simply fell through the dome in the Reading Room,' Tamaika said, curtailing Cador's meandering thoughts.

'Ah.' Cador paused. 'I don't believe Figrid simply fell. I believe he was lured and then pushed. I keep going back to *Rift Enchantress*. The description of the enchantress fits Mithla to a tee.'

'I fail to see any connection.'

'As would most,' Cador admitted. 'But it's almost as though the very act of writing about Mithla has somehow given life to her.'

'And yet she too is only a folk tale,' Tamaika reminded him.

'I have seen both the Hakogna and Mithla with

my own eyes,' Cador said. He sat back, almost expecting laughter.

But Tamaika was far from humour.

'I'm told *Rift Enchantress* is a bestseller,' Cador said. 'No one can explain its success. I suspect that people are too afraid to indulge in their usual entertainments out of doors. The citizenry are in need of a heroine in these dark times. And I'm glad to say it's a darn good book beside all that.'

Tamaika smiled fleetingly. 'A success,' she heard herself say.

'The most talked about author since Brice Daggersure,' Cador said. 'But an enigma. I would love to meet her.'

'Dacy Dunnard is actually …'

'Sorry Tamaika,' Cador interrupted. 'Yes, G'ladd?'

The deputy had appeared at the door. He beckoned Cador outside. 'Your brother, Chief Constable.'

'I'll be with you in one moment,' Cador told Tamaika.

Tamaika sat wringing her hands. Did she really want the world to know that she was Dacy Dunnard? Her sisters would be merciless. She would be hounded from her beloved library and there was her father to consider. But the happiness that was welling up inside her needed expression.

Maxon walked into Cador's office then, followed by G'ladd. Wearing the same uniform, minus the chief constable's armband which Tamaika failed to notice, Maxon went straight to Cador's bookshelf and pulled out a book on myths. He gave Tamaika a cursory glance and Tamaika saw him curl his upper lip in distaste.

What did I do wrong? she worried, mistaking Maxon for Cador.

Maxon turned back to G'ladd. 'Here's a picture of Mithla,' he said, stabbing his finger at a woodcut illustration. 'I'm offering twenty gold royals to anyone who finds her.' He looked at G'ladd and saw surprise on the deputy's face. 'I'm smitten by the woman,' he said. 'I have to find her.'

Tamaika started at these words. Flustered, she rushed from the room.

Cador returned to the office. 'Maxon, there you are. I see you've found the book. But there's a much more detailed description of her at the library.'

'Then you won't mind if I borrow this one?' Maxon said.

Cador shook his head, his mind elsewhere. 'Did you see a girl sitting here a moment ago?'

'I didn't notice,' Maxon said. To G'ladd he repeated, 'Twenty gold royals.'

The Chosen One

TAMAIKA SAT CROSS-LEGGED BENEATH her attic window listening to her sisters' incessant squabbling. It was dark outside and ominously quiet. She had long since given herself over to the entity that inhabited her body each night. Although she had absolutely no control over what happened to her during these visitations, she knew that somehow, Mithla's possession seemed to leave behind some kind of residue. Others noted it as well — most notably her sisters, who were even now arguing as to who should sweep the floor and clear away the dishes.

'Into the kitchen, you little tramp!' Byra had thundered earlier that night.

Tamaika smiled, remembering the look on Byra's wart-ridden face when Tamaika had simply ignored her and climbed the stairs to her attic. It had been a tiring day. Someone had been down in the cellar, clearly searching for something. The room had looked as though a cyclone had torn through it. Obviously the search had intended to uncover the *Princess of Shadows*. Somehow, it had remained hidden.

Seemingly at the thought of the book, the air around Tamaika condensed into a kind of fog, which started to swirl about, engulfing her. Once frightened at the transformation, she now willingly allowed Mithla to occupy her body. Energy surged through her. Mithla uncurled herself from the floor and swung up through the attic. Sniffing the air and her ears pricked for menacing sounds, she scraped her way up the chimney and down the other side. She prowled the city's finest buildings, those that housed the once dormant Hakogna.

Quentaris was mostly in darkness these nights. Many windows were blacked out, for fear that light drew attention. Mithla didn't have long to wait. She spied a host of Hakogna stomping across the rooftops, moving like ogres, their heavy cudgels ugly extensions of their ape-like arms. Like a shark in the night, Mithla stalked them.

She followed the creatures for an hour. They seemed to have an uncanny knack of knowing where the chief constable's men were. But magic did that, Mithla reminded herself. Presently she was waiting for the host to move on, but then they split into two groups. She chose one and followed it to a ware-house tenement in the wharf district. Confused, she delved into Tamaika's mind, seeking information.

Finding the place she sought only made her more puzzled. This was a poor part of the city, where wharf jacks and fishermen lived in cramped squalor. She hastened now, for already one of the Hakogna had pounded a hole in the shingles.

Dogs barked manically and an alarm was pealing.

Mithla landed beside the last of the Hakogna as it was about to plunge after its fellows. Its obsidian eyes flared with recognition but too late. Mithla's sword whistled as it lopped the creature's head. She knew it would reform soon but it would be out of action for the rest of this night at least.

With scarcely a thought, Mithla dropped through the hole in the roof.

The Hakogna had wasted no time. They had

cleared the entire floor of residents. They simply walked through the walls and batted the heavy doors aside. Amidst the din were cries of terror.

Mithla engaged another Hakogna. It stamped toward her, its footfalls shaking the boards beneath its feet. Hefting its great cudgel, the Hakogna swung it at her. The weapon swept above Mithla's head, clipping her hood, but the momentum of the cudgel spun the creature off balance. Mithla hacked at its legs, taking one out from beneath it and slicing a chunk from the other.

The Hakogna flailed its arms, trying to keep its balance, then toppled like a felled tree.

Mithla leapt over the struggling creature and sought its fellows. Her feet barely touching the stairs, she descended to the second level where a wall exploded inwards. Mithla stepped forward, not waiting for the dust to settle. As she predicted, a Hakogna pounded through the cloud. Her sword already raised, she swung down, cleaving its granite head. The creature staggered for a moment, wrenching Mithla's sword from her hand. Its head split, the Hakogna swung around blindly, its cudgel knocking aside falling debris.

Mithla waited for the cudgel to pass, then nimbly

rushed forward, drawing her sword free from the creature's head. She ducked as it swung its arms around, but in her haste she stumbled. Sensing its chance, the Hakogna reached down, grabbing her tunic in a vice-like grip.

Mithla was lifted like a rag doll and hurled against a retaining wall. She smashed through its lath and plaster, and rolled across the floor to cushion her fall. Dazed, Mithla needed time to regroup. She concentrated on the heavy wooden beam above the rampaging Hakogna. With more energy than she had to spare, she muttered an ancient spell. '*Ecceadvocare.*'

The tree-trunk-sized beam shattered as the Hakogna strode beneath it. Suddenly the roof caved in, burying the creature beneath a ton of rubble.

Coughing, Mithla struggled back from the deluge until she hit the wall behind her. The next moment she was hauled from the ground by the last Hakogna.

The life almost crushed from her, she was saved by a moment of clarity. She pushed with all her might and the Hakogna smashed through the warehouse window, taking her with it.

The pair plummeted to the docks below. The

Hakogna's weight sent them straight through the wooden pier into the icy depths below. Mithla struggled against the Hakogna's stony death grip. Sinking like the rock it was, the Hakogna plunged with its cargo to the riverbed.

On impact, the Hakogna's left arm shattered against a pylon. Mithla swam frantically. Breaking the surface, she gulped in a lungful of air and clung to a boat ramp. Spent, she somehow eluded the many patrols scouring the city and made it home to bed before first light.

Tamaika woke from a feverish dream. Sitting up in her bed, she could hardly believe how sore and weary her body felt. Although her body had become firm and her muscles taut, she had not the energy to move.

She dragged herself wearily off the pallet. She desperately needed more sleep, but something was pulling at her to get up and go to the library. Ordinarily she would not have minded, but right now Tamaika resisted the calling. Compelled, she found herself standing anyway. 'Well, why ever not?'

she mumbled. 'My life is no longer mine anyway.'

Getting dressed in itself was a painstaking business, but at last she dragged herself downstairs.

Byra was in the pantry. She turned and scowled at the sight of Tamaika. 'So you're up, are you?' she snapped. 'Get in here and prepare breakfast. Just because Father's not here doesn't mean you can slacken off. We've been much too lenient with you, you little scallywag!'

'Byra,' Tamaika said in a voice that seemed to be another's, 'it's too early for your nonsense.'

'Nonsense?' Byra spluttered.

Gabra and Hetta marched into the room then.

'We've taken just about as much as we can,' Gabra began.

'Fine, then I'll see you all later,' Tamaika said. Adding insult to injury, she snatched an apple from Byra's unresisting hand, took a huge chunk from it and nonchalantly munching it to the core, she left for work.

She arrived at the library at the seventh hour to be met by Head Librarian Tomes. The usually stern woman almost cowered at the sight of Tamaika climbing the steps.

'Tamaika,' Head Librarian Tomes said. 'You

have been summoned by the Six. Do you know of whom I speak?'

Tamaika's heart thudded. No one had ever met the six doyennes of the Great Library. In most quarters they were thought to be a myth to keep lower grade librarians in check. The look in Head Librarian Tomes's eyes dismissed Tamaika's doubts.

She nodded glumly. When was this nightmare going to end?

'Very well, then,' Head Librarian Tomes said. 'Follow me.'

The head librarian led Tamaika to the crypt where the Great Library's most treasured books were held. Visitors were allowed in here only under strict supervision and only the library's most trusted staff gained admittance.

Head Librarian Tomes locked the ironclad door and moved swiftly to a shelf at the back of the crypt. Tamaika was too overcome to see the chief custodian pull a latch. The laden bookshelf swung open like a door and Head Librarian Tomes beckoned Tamaika through it.

Lighting a torch, Head Librarian Tomes pulled down on a latch and the bookshelf closed behind them. Although Tamaika prided herself on knowing every inch of the library — certainly her sisters had commanded her to clean every inch — Tamaika had had no idea this passageway existed. It felt as though this place had been built when the very first stones of Quentaris were laid.

The flickering light on Head Librarian Tomes's face made her look spectral. 'Ordinarily, Tamaika, I would be bound to blind you momentarily. But it seems you are a Chosen One. Follow me carefully and do not veer from my path.'

Tamaika shadowed Head Librarian Tomes down a spiralling stone stairway. Had her mind been clear enough, Tamaika would have recognised some of the ward spells the Head was muttering as she weaved her way through various traps set by the Six.

Finally, they were on the threshold of a small hall. Guttering torches gave the room an orange glow. When Tamaika's eyes became accustomed to the dim light, she noticed a dais at one end, on which sat five women of indeterminate age.

'Come closer, child,' one of them said. 'My voice is no longer as strong as it once was.'

Head Librarian Tomes fluttered her hands, indicating Tamaika should obey immediately.

Tamaika looked up at the seated women. She

recognised three of them — C'sear, Tastr and Zar — as lifelong library members. They were particularly cantankerous and rarely had a nice word to say. The others were unknown to her. It was one of the strangers who spoke.

'My name is Hiseria,' she said. 'We are the guardians of the library — the Six — and we know what is happening to you.'

Sensing a certain animosity, Tamaika said, 'I'm not sure I understand.' She looked around for the sixth guardian.

The five ancients looked at one another, three scowling and two nodding approvingly. Hiseria said, 'It is well you keep the secret. There are those in the world who would see you undone.' She looked along the ranks of her colleagues. As one they all turned and gazed at Tamaika.

She stood firm. Once she would have wilted under such attention. Now she stared back. 'Why did the book choose me?' Her voice held a note of command.

Hiseria's brow arched and she chuckled. 'Uppity, aren't we, all of a sudden? Well, the book chooses a librarian of fortitude, of … virtue. You have been blessed, though you might not always think so.

Mithla has not appeared for well over a century. Once our peril is over, she will return to the book which will be lost till the next crisis beckons her.'

'I do not feel worthy,' Tamaika admitted.

'Exactly my point,' said Zar.

C'sear cleared her throat noisily. 'The book has clearly chosen wrongly,' she said. 'Never in the long history of heroines has one of such low office become the champion of Quentaris.'

'We should vote on this immediately,' snapped Tastr. She leaned forward. 'Just where have you hidden the book, Tamaika?'

Before she could respond, Hiseria said, 'A vote is out of order!'

Tamaika took a deep breath. A vote would clearly see her defeated three to two. Despite her self doubts, she wanted to be Mithla, Princess of Shadows. Being host to such a mighty warrior woman made her feel … special.

Someone clapped their hands and the sound reverberated around the hall. Tamaika looked up, but the five women were looking behind her. Tamaika turned slowly and saw Head Librarian Tomes standing. She was the sixth member of the group!

'There will be no vote,' the head librarian said. 'The book has chosen. Or have you forgotten your lore? Our sole purpose is to give aid to the Chosen One, the champion. Not to air our petty grievances.'

Tamaika couldn't believe her ears. Head Librarian Tomes, vouching for her!

'The First One has spoken,' Hiseria said, relieved. Head Librarian Tomes inclined her head.

She took the sixth seat and reached out and sought the hands of those sitting to either side of her. The others reluctantly linked hands, although three of the five did so unwillingly. They closed their eyes and began chanting.

Tamaika could not be sure, but her body seemed to tremble with a pulsing energy. She didn't know how long she stood there, mesmerised by the women's chanting.

Her reverie broke when Head Tomes laid a hand on her shoulder. 'It is done,' the Head said. 'Come along, before they recover.'

When they reached the top of the stairway, Tamaika said, 'Recover from what?'

Head Tomes hurried her through the open bookshelf. 'Some of our number were worried that you were not up to the duties bestowed upon you. It was decided to bring you before them for an accounting — and a joining if appropriate.' She smiled ruefully as the bookshelf slid shut. 'Knowing the power of Mithla, I can well imagine why some members of our order would wish to be chosen by the book. Such wanting has the power to corrupt.

'You must go now, Tamaika. And remember child, Mithla's ability to save Quentaris is reliant on her host's virtue. You must love Quentaris, first and foremost, else Mithla will desert us.'

10

Dacy Dunnard Exposed

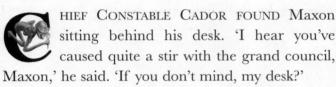HIEF CONSTABLE CADOR FOUND Maxon sitting behind his desk. 'I hear you've caused quite a stir with the grand council, Maxon,' he said. 'If you don't mind, my desk?'

Maxon relinquished the chair and smirked. 'Lord Chalm has promised the re-ennoblement of House Mercutis.'

'*If* you deliver that which you promise,' Cador reminded him. 'I hear you claim to have found a sorcerer who can stop these nightly depredations. How can one succeed when our best magicians have failed miserably?'

'Dearest brother,' Maxon said, pausing at the door, 'I made a promise over Mother's grave. I intend to fulfil that promise by whatever means necessary.'

There were no attacks on Quentaris that night; nor for several nights after. It seemed that Maxon was delivering, though how he managed it, Cador did not know. Dark suspicions came to his mind, but he tried to put them from him, for his father's sake.

Word soon spread, however, that it had been Maxon who had single-handedly saved Quentaris from the nightly scourge. The Archon was quick to seize upon the city's fervour. He declared the House Mercutis be given new status. Further, he appointed Maxon the new commander of the defences of Quentaris — a station above that of Commander Storm and Chief Constable Cador.

Cador sat glumly behind his desk. In just under a week, Maxon had requisitioned half of his armoury and seconded the best members of his constabulary. Worse, it appeared that his twin's own carefully selected men had been elevated to key positions in government, the military and even the banks, left vacant by those turned to stone by the Hakogna.

There had been two minor attacks over the past two nights and at first these had particularly worried

Cador. Ordinary citizens had been turned to stone — commoners who had no connection to Maxon whatsoever. But if Maxon hadn't planned it, he could not have wished for a better outcome. Attacks on the public had increased the level of panic. Rich merchants and nobles being turned to stone hardly worried the general populace. But now that they lay personally exposed to the plague …

The Archon had increased Maxon's powers to defend the common folk. His twin had become a despot overnight, declaring martial law and a curfew. Taxes were raised, poor people were evicted from their tenements and the rich were getting richer daily. And anyone who spoke out against him either disappeared or was charged with treason and imprisoned.

Disquieted, Cador wondered if he was the only one who had noticed Maxon's meteoric rise to power. Soon, he would be more powerful than the Archon himself. But it would be too late then to turn the tide of events. Maxon was already too influential to topple easily. No one dared speak out against him. It was said he now controlled most of the major guilds, the newspapers, and yes, Quentaris itself.

Cador felt drained. He shoved his precious

reports from the desk. So much for his theories concerning the Hakogna and Mithla. It appeared that Dacy Dunnard and any connection with Tamaika Erskona were entirely erroneous as well. As for *Rift Enchantress* … Cador shook his head. All one big red herring. But how could his brother have solved a problem that eluded the city's greatest magicians and minds?

Pondering this conundrum, Cador sat behind his desk well into the night.

Tamaika stretched out on her pallet, her stomach knotted. Despite the various remedies concocted for her by a herbalist, the pain would not abate. Why had Mithla deserted her? The Hakogna had not attacked in force for two weeks now, but the menace was still lurking. Head Librarian Tomes's warning about loving Quentaris first and foremost resonated in her mind. She loved Cador of course, but the feeling was not reciprocated. Had Mithla sensed her unrequited love?

She tossed from side to side in misery. How she missed those nights roaming the rooftops, the thrill of the chase, the scent of her prey. Tamaika's eyes closed and she drifted to sleep.

It seemed as though she had just put her head upon the pillow when she awoke. Something was different. Against all hope she reached down and her fingers closed around the hilt of her sword. Looking down even as her consciousness withdrew, Tamaika realised that she had become the Princess of Shadows.

Mithla hauled herself through the attic window. She sniffed the air, tasting the disparate scents and smells on the wind. There were no Hakogna on the prowl this night — her prey was rather more mortal. Leaping across the narrow alleyways she moved briskly across town until she had reached the docks.

Crouching like one of the Hakogna, she rested above a squad of Maxon's militia.

'Move along now,' bawled a sergeant. 'It's for your own safety. The Hakogna are on the loose.'

A woman and her two children refused to be evicted. 'This is our home. We should defend it, not run,' she screamed. 'Where's the City Watch? Under what authority?'

Others joined in. Soon, five or six residents were jostling and arguing with the militia. 'I demand to see the chief constable!' a tenant shrieked as she was manhandled from a warehouse that had been converted to dwellings.

'Right, lads,' the sergeant said. 'I sense rebellion. Let them have what for.'

His men withdrew their batons and charged the resisting tenants.

No one saw the shadowy shape as it appeared to slide across the warehouse wall. From window to window it swept, hands and feet magically adhering to pitted stone with spider-like agility, before leaping to adjacent tenements. Mithla reached the street and darted forward through the darkness, her speed a blur of motion to any casual onlooker.

Before two militiamen knew about it, an irresistible force hauled them back by the scruff of their necks. With one quick flick of her gloved hands, Mithla cracked their heads together, letting them drop to the wooden pier like sacks of cement. No doubt they would have blistering headaches for several days to come.

Mithla felled two more militiamen before their fellows realised she was amongst them, yet not until they had drawn their swords did she unsheathe hers. They charged forward, but in their haste they bunched up, leaving themselves little room to manoeuvre.

Mithla dispatched those who came within reach of her sword and deftly disposed of two who were craftier than their fellows and tried to flank her. Three ran off, leaving the sergeant to confront the costumed warrior alone.

He hefted his sword, then hesitated, gazing around at the bodies of his men lying in a scraggly heap. His thirst for a fight quickly faded. 'Next time,' he said, backing away. Then he broke into a run and raced after his men, loudly cursing them for cowards.

The evictees cheered, but Mithla did not stay to hear their thanks. She quickly scaled a drainpipe and was soon lost among the rooftop shadows.

The woman with the two children watched her go, shaking her head. 'You see that?' she said to a plump man nearby, one of her neighbours. 'That was the Princess of Shadows herself.'

'Can't be,' said the man. 'I heard the princess was in league with the stone people.'

'Maybe she is and maybe she ain't,' said the woman, 'but she ain't in league with this rotten lot!' She glared at the senseless militiamen, then spat on them.

Maxon thumped Cador's desk with his fist. 'Five times this masked woman has interfered with the Archon's business,' he thundered.

Cador's mouth twitched with barely concealed delight. 'You mean *your* business, don't you, Maxon? Besides, your propaganda machine has been at work. I hear tell that half of Quentaris believes that she's the villain here and not you.'

Maxon started to retort, then stopped himself. He eyed his twin brother. 'You would do well not to provoke me, brother dearest,' he said in a silky tone that Cador knew spelled danger. 'It is the Archon's wish that I make Quentaris safe from this … malady that has stricken us. The docks, as everyone knows, are particularly vulnerable to attack for they are farthest from the barracks. I merely wish to relocate the people there to where they'll be safer.'

'And yet two of the demolished warehouses are being refurbished by some nebulous merchant. A Bruntian it is rumoured. Or maybe someone from Tolrush. Many wonder who sponsors the project and who will reap the profits.'

'Keep to matters that concern you,' Maxon said

darkly. 'Now, what of the money this masked crusader has stolen?'

'By all accounts,' Cador said, 'it's only being stolen from your coffers, and promptly redistributed to the people who had it stolen from them in the first place.'

Maxon's face went deathly still. 'Taxes, dear brother, are what make a city great. As for this ridiculous myth that the Princess of Shadows steals from the rich and gives to the poor … no one is so magnanimous.'

'What is it that you want from me, Maxon?' Cador asked, enjoying his brother's frustration.

'I want this — this charlatan — found. I want her brought to justice. You're the chief constable. Get your people out there and find her.'

Cador raised his hands, palms outward in a helpless gesture.

'If I had anyone left I surely would,' Cador said. 'But you see, my hands are tied.' He looked down at himself, at his plain tunic and unembroidered breeches, and smiled. He had forsworn wearing his uniform, for he had soon realised that Maxon's watchers spotted him too easily and followed his every move, attempting what disguise and concealment they could. Of course, his own people watched the watchers, but Maxon did not need to know that.

His brother strode to the door and turned abruptly, stabbing his finger at Cador. 'You will be relieved of duty unless she is found, Cador. Believe me, I will ruin you if I have to.'

Cador watched Maxon collect his personal guard and cross the street. He pondered his own predicament for a moment. He would gladly give up his position, only he was of more help to Quentaris as the chief constable than he would be brooding in the city's dungeons, or left on the sidelines while others laboured.

He buckled his sword belt and went for a stroll, unaware that he was moving in the direction of the library. Fresh air often cleared his mind and the mindless rhythm of walking allowed him to think. Right now he very much needed to consider every piece of this puzzle.

More and more he believed the ancient stone gargoyles, the Hakogna, to be the source of the scourge affecting Quentaris, but Maxon — and through him the Archon, supposedly — jeered at the notion, accusing him of an infatuation with childhood fairy tales. The more he insisted that the Hakogna were at the heart of this matter, the more he risked being publicly disgraced and sacked. The ridicule at court had effectively sealed his lips, but it had not stopped his investigation. He was merely more discreet about it.

Each night he positioned men to watch the remaining stone statues peopling the rooftops, gables and turrets of Quentaris, but so far no one but Cador and Maxon had seen a Hakogna come to life. Nor was there any mystery in this. There were hundreds of Hakogna left in their eyries and only a few dozen watchmen.

Of course, statistically, one of them should have seen something.

But they didn't.

Which meant they were weren't supposed to. Whatever magic reanimated the mighty stone beasts, it had some awareness of prying eyes. To be certain, Cador had secretly sought out a foreign wizard — one who might be expected to have formed few loyalties as yet in Quentaris — and asked if such magic would be difficult.

'Is nothing, this,' said the earth wizard, laughing. 'In my country, boys do this. When teacher looks away, chalk writes on blackboard behind back. He turn round, is normal again, no matter how quick. Is very funny.'

So the mystery was a little less mysterious. Yet it meant that he could offer little in the way of proof for his theory. Which left him pretty much back where he started. Besides, according to his men, the gargoyles he had dismantled were no longer to be found. He shivered at this thought. There was an army out there that he himself had helped build.

Cador came out of his reverie and stared about. He was not far from the library, which was odd. He hadn't meant to come this way at all. He looked around and was shocked to see Tamaika sitting on a fountain in the Square of Dreams not twenty feet away. The blood mounted to his face in a furious blush, but she was not looking in his direction thankfully. What is happening to me? he wondered. Am I … am I in love with this girl? If his pulse rate was anything to go by, then it was a resounding yes.

He stared at her, entranced. He had never noticed how lovely she was before. Her face, in profile, was delicately shaped, and her hair, swept back as it was today, was like a mane. He had a strange desire to run his fingers through that hair.

Cador started to turn away, feeling unaccountably awkward, then he stopped, berating himself for a fool. He took several deep breaths, steeled himself to be calm, and sat down beside her, affecting a casualness he was alarmed to realise was utterly false. He said, as evenly as he could, 'Quentaris looks quite magnificent on a sunny day.'

He cringed inwardly. Quentaris looks quite magnificent on a sunny day? Where in the bowels of Quentaris did he get a phrase like that? From some silly romance play at the local theatre? By all the gods he would be stuttering like a schoolboy next.

Tamaika looked up, startled at Cador's voice. Immediately her heart started to thump and she was confused. The memory of Cador ignoring her and beseeching his deputy to find Mithla was still raw, yet there were other conflicting feelings as well.

She stood up in a fluster. 'I'm late for work,' she said. 'I must get back.'

Cador also stood, feeling just as flustered. 'Wait, please don't go. Sit with me a moment.'

Despite her rising panic, Tamaika put down her hessian bag. 'For a moment.'

They both sat down, keeping a careful distance between them. Cador, who rarely was at a loss for words, felt quite tongue-tied. He was also confused. Tamaika had seemed quite keen on him at one point, but now she was cool and remote. 'Thank you,' he muttered, then regretted the tone of his voice in case she thought it was directed at her.

He gazed at the markets and street vendors. A nearby bookseller gave him a topic to pursue. 'How fares *Rift Enchantress* in the public opinion? I'm afraid I haven't had time to ask anyone.'

Tamaika looked down at her hands, realised she was wringing them fretfully, and stopped. 'I hear it is doing very well. It has gone into another reprint.'

'Then we can expect a sequel?'

'I suppose,' said Tamaika. Did he know she was the author, or was this just polite chitchat? 'I believe most of the popular authors provide sequels.'

'It is something to look forward to,' he said with genuine fervour. 'I'm sure the second will be as unputdownable as the first.' This disarmed her somewhat. It was heady stuff, hearing accolades from an enthusiast, even if that person didn't know he was talking to the author. Come to think of it, it was even better that way.

She forced herself to inquire about his investigation. It seemed rude not to. He told her about his theory concerning the Hakogna and the reaction to this theory at court. Then he sighed.

'It is a pleasure to talk to you,' he said. 'I don't have anyone to confide in.' He glanced at her, wondering if he had said too much. 'May I continue?'

Tamaika nodded briefly, not trusting herself to speak. His nearness made her feel giddy.

Cador made sure they could not be overheard. 'I have — suspicions. Concerning my brother, Maxon.' He hesitated. Should he confide in her? Yet he must speak to someone and she seemed so honest and safe. 'I suspect him of treason,' he blurted out. 'I'm probably alone in saying this, but Maxon has always been an ambitious one. The low prestige of our House gave him, even as a child, great bitterness and resentment. Always he dreamed of making House Mercutis great again, rivalling the Duelphs and Nibhellines. Becoming a player at court and gaining access to the rift caves, and all the riches and potential power they promise. I confess that I fear where his loyalties now lie.'

'Your own brother?' Tamaika asked in amazement.

'Good ol' Maxon, yes,' Cador said. 'Right now my brother basks in the glory of having rid the city of its nemesis — seemingly.'

'You think the attacks will return?'

'I think the source of them has never left us.'

'Can you prove this?' Tamaika said.

'Ah, therein lies the rub, Tamaika,' he said. 'I have no evidence other than my lifelong knowledge of his ways. He has never been one to be altruistic. No, I fear that whatever he is seeking will spell ruin and pain for us all.'

'Yet you do not openly accuse him, only in these whispers to me.'

Cador shrugged. 'I guess he's still my brother.'

'What will you do, Cador?'

He stared at her. It was the first time she had used his name. 'I … I need to find the Princess of Shadows — if she's real and not just a hallucination. Others are also looking for her and if they find her first … What's wrong, Tamaika? Are you ill?'

Tamaika had gone very still, the colour draining from her face. Memory rushed back, Cador telling his deputy to find the woman he was besotted by at all costs, ignoring her completely. Before Tamaika knew what she was doing, she had leapt to her feet and was hurrying away across the square. Dimly she heard Cador call out to her. It spurred her on even faster. She did not want him to see the tears streaming down her face.

'Your carry-all!' Cador called, clutching Tamaika's hessian bag. Already she was lost in the throng of the mid afternoon crowd. He sat back down, wondering what he had said wrong.

Feeling stupid and clumsy, he looked down at

Tamaika's bag. Inside was a bundle of neatly tied parchment. Gently untying the ribbon, he saw that it was a handwritten manuscript. Scarcely believing his eyes, he read out aloud, *Return of the Rift Enchantress*, by Dacy Dunnard. Momentarily confused, he unravelled another piece of parchment, obviously a shopping list. With dawning comprehension, he compared the identical handwriting.

'Tamaika is Dacy Dunnard,' he whispered. Despite his shock, Cador tucked Tamaika's shopping bag beneath his arm and pressed forward through the crowd.

Within a half hour he was breathlessly facing Head Librarian Tomes. 'I need to see Tamaika,' he said.

'As do I,' Head Librarian Tomes said. 'No one has seen her since she left here some hours ago.'

Cador turned to leave.

'Chief Constable?' she called.

Cador turned.

'Ensure her safety, won't you? There are those who would harm her.'

'With my life,' Cador said without hesitation. But why would Maxon wish to hurt Tamaika? he wondered.

The Creature Odessar

HANDS CLUTCHED BEHIND HIS back, Maxon strode along a row of his lieutenants as they stood to attention, not daring to breathe. 'I want the docklands cleared, do you hear me, fools? I want everyone out. If your men are afraid to go down there in the dark, then have them do it in broad daylight. But get it done or I'll send you through the Medoid rift cave.'

His assembled officers stirred uneasily. The banned Medoid rift cave led to a world where the very soil was said to turn one's flesh leprous. It was sealed by a metal door two feet thick that was always shut.

'Begging your pardon, sir,' said the newly promoted Lieutenant G'ladd, somewhat nervously, 'but to evict the tenants during the day would bring down the wrath of the people. There would be anarchy in the streets.'

Maxon stalked over to the lieutenant. 'Well and good, G'ladd. I will hold you personally responsible for a midnight raid.' He glared briefly at the rest of his officers. 'I hereby place you all under the direct command of *Major* G'ladd. I want every able-bodied man and woman down there tonight. You will capture this Mithla, Princess of Shadows, and you will bring her back alive.'

'Now get out of my sight.'

They quickly filed out, bunching up at the door like schoolboys trying to escape a wrathful head-master.

Maxon cursed beneath his breath. How could one woman elude his every attempt to capture her? Well, there was one more lure he would use to bait the so-called Princess of Shadows. With that thought he marched down to the guardhouse dungeon where a special cell had been constructed. Guards were stationed at an outer cell door. He unlocked this, stepped through and locked it behind him again, then strode down a long, dark corridor towards a flaring torch. Here he turned left, coming to another locked door. He unlocked this, descended some stairs and stopped in front of a solitary cell.

The smell in the confined space was nearly intolerable. Maxon had chosen this cellar not for its pleasing aspects, but for its isolation.

He stared in at the pathetic creature manacled to the cold bluestone wall. Half human, half beast, the creature growled deeply at the human. Twisted and bent with age, crippled by a recent ailment, his eyes nonetheless were black chips of hate, and very much alive.

'Well you might loathe me, my pet,' Maxon gloated, 'but for as long as you are fettered by raw iron, so your allegiance will be to me. Remember, Odessar, on a whim I can destroy you — a fact you should think on.'

At Odessar's baleful silence, Maxon continued. 'Tonight you will resurrect an army of Hakogna. They will swarm over Quentaris like a plague. They will reach the Archon's palace. And they will spare no one therein. Do you understand, beast? Not turned to stone. They are all to die.'

The prisoner lunged to the full length of his shackles, his clawed hands barely reaching the bars of the cell. He spat at Maxon.

Maxon kicked at him savagely through the bars, breaking some of his talons.

'Then I die!' Odessar said sibilantly. His voice

was like an echo from another world. There was a tiny delay between the movement of the lips and the sound reaching Maxon's ears. He had never gotten used to it.

'Not until I see the Nibhellines and the Duelphs finished,' Maxon said. 'Only then shall you have the death you crave.'

He eyed Odessar with distaste and not a little horror.

'This Princess of Shadows. Tell me why she is to be feared. Tell me now. I will not be put off further, beast!' He shook the bars. 'I have done as you suggested. Half the city searches for her. Now explain how a mere girl is a mortal danger to me.'

Odessar hissed at him. 'Not mere girl,' he rasped. 'Spirit of this city.'

'Enough foolish riddles,' snarled Maxon. 'Tell me straight. Who must I truly fear?'

Odessar's sunken eyes blinked slowly. 'Quentaris,' he said. 'Quentaris is thy enemy.'

12

Maxon Springs His Trap

A S CADOR APPROACHED TAMAIKA'S street he saw Maxon's men on the corner, leaning on their pikes, laughing and calling out to the passers-by, especially the prettier girls. An old man shuffled past, taking his time, 'Move on there, you doddering fool,' said one of the men and he helped the old man with a boot to the seat of his pants. The old man fell over.

A young girl went to his assistance, glaring at the men. 'You should have more respect,' she said.

They laughed. One of them made a lewd gesture. 'You want some respect? Come with me and I'll show you respect.'

The girl sniffed as haughtily as she could and helped the frail man down the street. Cador had ducked into a doorway as soon as he saw the guards and he watched them now. They were new recruits, unfamiliar to him, but he could not take the risk that they might recognise him. If he was seen entering Tamaika's building the information would get back to Maxon and Cador knew his brother only too well.

Maxon's curiosity would be piqued.

Cador pulled a hood over his head, blended with the crowd, and drifted past the watchmen, keeping his face averted. When he got to the next corner he ducked down an alleyway. There would be guards in the next street, too, he realised — part of the city-wide martial law — which meant that the best entry was the unexpected one. Luckily evening was coming on fast. Cador stacked several refuse boxes beneath a window. Standing on top of them, he could reach the ornate sill if he jumped. If he missed, he would fall back into the alleyway — not a great drop, but one that would attract attention. Gathering himself, he crouched and sprang. His hands grasped at the sill, but it was slippery with moss. For a moment, he clung tenaciously by one hand, then managed to swing up with all his might, hook his other hand over the ledge and hold on.

Scrabbling with his feet against the brickwork, he got one elbow onto the sill, then levered himself up till he was crouched on the wide window ledge.

Although the shutters were closed, he was pretty sure that no one was in the parlour. Sliding the blade of his service knife between the dual shutters, he managed to unlatch the catch. Quickly, he climbed inside. Immediately, he swept through the downstairs rooms. With only the attic space unaccounted for, he made for the stairs.

Poking his head through the trap door, he stopped, transfixed. Tamaika was on the floor, shaking like a rag doll coming to life. He rushed toward her, even as her clothes shimmered like a heat haze and the raiment of Mithla, the Princess of Shadows, replaced them.

Cador staggered back. He let Tamaika's hessian bag fall from his numb fingers. Finally, he half sat, half collapsed on the pallet.

Mithla sat up. Instantly aware of his presence she sprang forward like a panther. Cador scrambled up even as Mithla was disappearing through the attic window. 'Wait!' he cried. Without thought, he grasped a hold of Mithla's booted foot.

She stayed caught for a moment, then with a flick of her foot eluded his grip. He pulled himself up, expecting to see her fleeing across the rooftops, but she was crouching like a feline ready to spring.

Cador saw several of Maxon's men prowling the rooftops. He beckoned Mithla back down, and surprisingly, she came.

Cador stood back when Mithla slipped through the window. 'No one must know the host of the Chosen One,' she said sorrowfully. 'He who covets her would control me and that is not permitted.'

She advanced towards Cador. His hand crept to his sword. The pommel felt comforting, but he knew that he would be no match for her.

'Tamaika need not fear me,' Cador said quickly. 'I … I love her.'

Mithla stopped, her head cocked like a querying dog's. 'Love?'

'Yes. I would give my life for her.'

Confusion swept Mithla's face.

Cador's back hit the attic wall. 'Tamaika, can you hear me? I wish you no harm, you know that. I will protect your secret.'

Mithla came close. Her hand snapped up and Cador flinched, but she unexpectedly stroked his cheek. Her touch was surprisingly gentle. 'You are very pretty,' she said. 'Does the girl love you?'

'I … don't know.'

Mithla rested her hand on his cheek and looked in his eyes. 'I remember love,' she said, with a kind of wistfulness that Cador did not understand. 'It seems like the memory of a dream of a story I once heard … so long ago.' It seemed to Cador that the very thought of love weakened her resolve.

She was lost in thought then her hand went to his throat and quickly closed about his windpipe, though she did not apply any pressure yet.

Cador's hand came up. He was holding *Rift Enchantress*. 'Tamaika. I've been a fool. You were right in front of me all along. Tamaika?'

'Tamaika isn't here, mortal. The ancient debt must be served. Quentaris is more than the life of one solitary being. Forgive me.'

Her hand tightened on his throat. 'Tamaika,' he gasped. 'Don't let her do this!' He tripped and stumbled backwards, slamming into the pallet, but Mithla's grip did not ease for a second. Although he fought against it, unconsciousness quickly claimed him. The last thing he saw was the face of Mithla, the Princess of Shadows, her eyes filled with tears of remorse.

Cador feebly slapped away the wet rag that was dabbing his forehead. In waking he thought it was his wolfhound, Molly, licking his face. 'What happened?' he croaked.

Tamaika's face leaned above him, smiling. Her eyes were wet. 'It's me,' she whispered. 'Hold still, there's some bruising.' Satisfied he was all right, she sat back.

Cador pushed himself up till he was resting with his back to the wall. 'What happened? Where's Mithla?'

Tamaika wiped at her eyes. 'She's gone. She was going to hurt you. I thought — that is — we struggled. Then Mithla realised that I cared more for you than I did for Quentaris.' Tamaika cleared her throat. 'She left, Cador. She's gone. And I've betrayed our city and the trust placed in me by a long line of librarian-heroines.'

She bowed her head and tears trickled down her cheeks. Cador reached out, lifted her face so he could look into her eyes. He leant forward and gently kissed the tears from her cheeks, tasting their saltiness.

Tamaika let out a tiny moan, tried half-heartedly to pull away. 'Don't,' she said in a whisper. 'I've betrayed everybody.'

He brought her face around and looked at her. Then he kissed her mouth, crushing her lips. And Tamaika felt something inside her give way, like a dam bursting, like a thing she had held in check her whole life. She realised she could not remember anyone ever loving her. She threw her arms around Cador's neck and returned his passionate kisses, all the time sobbing as if she had been deeply wounded, or as if some deep wound were only now being healed.

Some long time later as they sat, arms still tightly wound around each other, Tamaika explained to him about the Six and what they had said and how now Mithla was gone and it was all her fault.

'Would you turn back the clock?' he asked gently. 'Would you change this?'

She buried her face against his neck. 'Not for anything,' she said. 'Not for anything.'

'Maxon is the real villain here, Tamaika. Not you.'

'But you don't understand,' Tamaika whispered. 'Without Mithla's help, Maxon can do anything he likes. She knew he was using some kind of powerful magic, the like of which has never been seen in Quentaris before. Mithla … she was so powerful!'

'Yet you overcame her.'

Tamaika looked at him, not understanding.

'You did it, Tamaika. You bested her. You chased her away to save me.'

'No, that wasn't me.'

'How do you know?'

'I couldn't have. I'm just a librarian.'

Cador laughed. 'Maybe librarians are more powerful than we imagine.'

'But Quentaris *needs* Mithla,' said Tamaika. 'It needs her strength.'

'How do you know that this wasn't supposed to happen?'

'What?'

'Did it ever occur to you that Mithla might not have reappeared in order to be the heroine that saves Quentaris?'

'But why else would she come?'

'To be the midwife.'

Tamaika stared at him. 'Why? To do what?'

'To make the heroine that saves Quentaris.'

Tamaika was too shocked to say anything. Cador picked up her manuscript. Riffling through the pages, he said, 'Anyone who can write a story such as this, has a great power of their own — power of the imagination.'

Tamaika got slowly to her feet and started pacing. Despite having lost Mithla, she still felt something of her inside, an echo, a shadow, a trace …

'I'm right, aren't I?' said Cador, watching her.

'I don't know. I don't know anything any more.'

'Perhaps if we …'

'Wait a minute,' said Tamaika. 'It's tonight, Cador. I can feel it. Mithla knew that tonight was the night. All shall be lost or won this night.'

'Then we must find the truth.'

'There is one person who knows the truth and who is probably behind all this.'

'Maxon?'

'Yes, him, but also the power behind him, the power that stopped the attacks. And probably also started them.'

'A powerful talisman? Something from the rifts?'

'A powerful sorcerer who has pledged himself to Maxon's cause, more likely,' said Tamaika.

'No one has seen such a sorcerer.'

'Then we must smoke him out,' said Tamaika.

'Easier said than done.'

Tamaika's eyes sparkled. 'Not if we spread the rumour that you have captured a live Hakogna.'

It didn't take long for Tamaika's friend, Tibbid, the town crier, to announce to the public that Chief Constable Cador had captured a gargoyle. Nor that its interrogation would be conducted forthwith.

The 'captured' Hakogna was making so much noise in its wooden crate that Cador felt compelled to tell it to rest easy.

'Sorry,' came the muffled reply from the crate in which one of his men was imprisoned.

Cador glanced nervously at his hand-picked men. They were the best of what was left of his constabulary. He had them spread across the nearby rooftops and down in the winding streets surrounding his barracks. They would have plenty of warning at least when the attack came. If it comes, he caught himself thinking.

He could see that Tamaika was unsure of herself too. She stood chewing her fingernails, the westering sun bathing her in an orange glow. Cador hadn't wanted Tamaika to be there, but she had insisted, blaming herself for the loss of Mithla.

When the attack came, it was not what they expected.

Maxon made an appearance almost as though by sleight of hand. He managed to slip by several look-outs and it was Tamaika whose keen sight saw his shadow spill into the room, backlit by the flaming torches outside. She didn't call out immediately, for she was stunned by the man's resemblance to Cador and suddenly understood what had happened in the office that day. She remembered this man glaring down at her, thinking it was Cador. 'He's here, Cador.'

Startled, Cador spun round, but recovered quickly.

'Congratulations, my dear brother,' Maxon said sweetly, coming into the room and inspecting the crate. 'Let us take a look at your captive. You understand that I must interrogate the creature immediately?'

Cador pulled his brother's hands from the crate. 'I'm afraid that's not possible, Maxon.'

'Unhand me,' Maxon said. He wrestled out of Cador's grip.

Without thinking, Cador said, 'Arrest him.'

Several constables sprang forward and within seconds Maxon was restrained.

'I'll see you hanged for this outrage, Cador,'

Maxon seethed. He stared around at his captors. 'All of you. For treason.'

Cador eyed his brother, feeling light-headed, as if he had stepped too close to the edge of a cliff. 'Now that it's come to this, Maxon, we must press on to the finish.' He nodded to his men to maintain their hold on the prisoner. 'I've guessed all along that you've had something to do with the Hakognas' resurrection.'

'You'll never prove a thing against me,' Maxon vowed. 'I'll have every one of your tongues out before the night's end.'

Cador thought there was a good chance of that. 'Maybe. But right now I wouldn't lay bets on it.' Good, that rang with some conviction. 'You've been exceedingly brilliant, Maxon. How did you do it? How did you bring Quentaris to her knees so rapidly?'

Maxon stopped struggling, and his fury seemed to slip from him, as if it had been feigned. 'It will do you no good to know, brother dearest.'

'Humour me, brother dearest.'

Maxon shrugged. 'It was easy, as you would know if you did anything other than read books. I had heard of a mighty rift sorcerer who could fashion magic like none had ever seen. The rumour of his deeds had travelled to many worlds and he was said to be a strange creature, not entirely human, but some half-breed thing. I tracked the beast through countless rifts and at last captured him. As we speak, he resides in the Archon's deepest dungeon.'

'Not such a mighty sorcerer,' Tamaika said, 'caught so easily by an adventurer.'

Maxon did not bother to look at her. 'During the hunt I discovered his weakness easily enough, by the worlds he avoided.' He snorted. 'But look at you brother, surrounded by your men and this puny girl. You're afraid, I can smell it oozing from you.'

'If I fear, brother, it is at what you have become, or what you always were. And at the disservice you have done to our once proud name,' Cador replied.

Maxon tensed. 'You always were a fool, Cador. It was you to whom Father looked to restore the prestige of House Mercutis. You who he lavished his attention and hopes upon. But it is I who has achieved his dream. House Mercutis will once again be a power to reckon with. All due to me!'

'You have brought us nothing but shame, Maxon,' Cador said sadly. 'And like many would-be despots, you confuse authority with power.'

'I *will* rule,' Maxon gloated. 'No matter what name you give it. Why, even as we speak, the Archon's palace is being breached by the Hakogna. By midnight, I will be supreme ruler of Quentaris. And let none mock the name of House Mercutis then!'

Cador saw his men's resolve weaken. Several had even taken steps back as though in obeisance. 'It will be a hollow victory I assure you,' he said. 'Put him in the crate as planned.'

Maxon held firm. 'You must think me a fool to walk into your childish little trap unprepared. Now that I have all the rats in my own trap, I shall spring it. To me, men!'

Half of Cador's men drew their swords. Caught completely unaware, his own loyal constables were slow to react. Two fell to sword thrusts before they could collect their wits.

Tamaika snatched up a fallen sword, even as Maxon grabbed another.

'Get away, Tamaika!' Cador cried, parrying a thrust from his twin.

Clanging swords resounded down in the alley-ways. Maxon's trap was well and truly sprung. A guard lunged at Tamaika. She whipped up her sword, buckling beneath the impact of the man's blow. As she stumbled, he raised his sword to strike her dead. Across the room, Cador saw this and knew that there was nothing he could do. Tamaika was defenceless, off balance and wide open.

'Tamaika!' he cried out.

But something in Tamaika had awakened. Whether from the Six, or the residue from Mithla, she never knew. Tamaika slumped, as if recognising her defeat. Her attacker paused a moment, savouring this moment. And that was his undoing. Tamaika kicked out at the man's groin and he doubled over.

She pushed him aside and steadied her sword.

Alarm bells were pealing. The Archon's palace bells. Tamaika made a quick decision. Those loyal to Cador were holding their own. Forgetting that she was no longer Mithla, she leapt through a window and landed like a cat on a lower roof. The fall scarcely slowed her. Soon she was sailing across an alleyway and was halfway across the next building's roof.

Odessar

TAMAIKA CROUCHED IN THE shadows of the Archon's palace. The battlements seemed oddly deserted. And no wonder, she thought. Maxon's in charge of the Archon's defences. Stepping over the mangled gates, Tamaika ran across the grassy courtyard and up the marble steps. The once imposing doors had been shattered and lay like kindling across the threshold.

Tamaika hesitated, taking in the damage.

A cudgel struck the step next to her. Had she moved an inch, the cudgel would have decapitated her. Its impact with the floor sent chips of marble slicing through the air.

Stumbling back, Tamaika drew her sword and with all her might struck at the lone Hakogna. Sparks flew as the sword rasped down its stone hide.

'Ugh!' she grunted at the impact.

The gargoyle hefted its cudgel and stalked after her, its footfalls pounding as it descended the stairs. Tamaika fled before its advance. A wolfhound loped across the gardens, but it bypassed Tamaika and snapped at the Hakogna which swiped at the animal. The wolfhound easily avoided the blow.

Free from pursuit, Tamaika climbed a drainpipe and clambered over a balcony. Smashing the window she moved quickly across the darkened parlour. Every room she passed had been destroyed. Furniture lay broken like firewood, draperies torn from their rails. Tamaika had no idea where the Archon's dungeons were, but she knew they had to be beneath the palace.

A scream ripped through the air. Tamaika's heart leapt with fear at the ferocity of that plea for help. She ran along the darkened corridor, following the now continuous screaming.

She stopped outside a bedchamber. A Hakogna had a scullery maid trapped behind a chest of drawers. Without thinking, Tamaika rushed forward and hacked at the creature's legs. Chips flew from its thighs and the being screeched as though wounded. It swung on Tamaika, its eyes seeking its tormentor.

'The door,' Tamaika screamed at the girl. 'Speed is our only defence. Quickly, now!'

The girl needed no second warning. She deftly sidestepped the Hakogna and joined Tamaika in the corridor. Clasping the girl's hand, Tamaika pulled her forward.

'I need the dungeons,' Tamaika said. 'Where are they?'

'What? What?' the maid shrieked. 'We need help! Where are the guards? We've been deserted.'

Tamaika stopped and slapped the maid across the face. Then cupping the hysterical girl's face, she said, 'Sorry, but I need to know where the dungeons are.'

The girl's eyes flickered, as though seeing Tamaika for the first time. 'The east wing,' she said, dazed. 'That way.'

'Listen to me,' Tamaika told her. She had to bring the maid's face around, for someone else was screaming somewhere in the palace. 'Get out of here. I can't stop these creatures unless I find someone. I need to go now.'

The girl clutched at her. 'Don't leave me!'

Tamaika disentangled herself from the maid's clasping hands. 'Run. I can't help you.' Tamaika didn't wait for the girl's response. She had to find the sorcerer before the entire household fell to the Hakogna.

Skirting several rampaging Hakogna, Tamaika finally located the dungeons. Not surprisingly, they were unguarded and the doors had been left open as though in haste. Without pause, she descended the stairs and was soon swallowed up by the gloom.

She lost count of the levels as she crossed the worn flagstones. Only her single-mindedness kept the dank and stale air at bay. She found the sorcerer in the deepest cellar. She saw that he was not a man, or not completely. Whatever he was, judging by his protruding ribs, he was half starved and had been tortured. Tamaika approached the cell warily, unsure whether the creature would aid her or oppose her. The suffocating air now closed in on her — it was like nothing she had ever breathed before.

As she came closer, the degradation of the creature's flesh became more apparent. Great open contusions seeped pus and crawled with maggots. The creature's flesh was putrefying as he lay there.

'Oh, I'm so sorry,' Tamaika whispered, blinking back tears.

Odessar lifted his sagging eyelids. In a paper-fine voice he said, 'I am Odessar. I sense power. You are *she* — who I asked for.'

Tamaika made the sign of her saviour. 'I don't …
I … what have they *done* to you?'

Odessar said, 'I am near death now.' He seemed
to see Tamaika's sorrow at this. 'My death not like
your death. Sorrow not.'

Tamaika found keys, a bundle of them on a thick
ring hanging on the wall. Jangling them before the
prisoner, she said, 'Which one? Quick, I can help
you.'

Odessar sighed heavily, but said, 'Big one. Brass.'

Tamaika fumbled with the key, unlocked the cell
door. It clanged open. Noises farther up the stairs
made her heart lurch. She was trapped down here
with no exit. 'The shackles. Which key?' She had to
bring the creature's face around to face her. 'Which
key?'

Again, Odessar indicated one. 'Important I die
free … No iron *iln*, no *shame*.'

Tamaika unlocked the shackles and dragged
Odessar from the cell. Ominous sounds were rever-
berating down the stairs. Stone grinding upon
stone …

She cradled Odessar's skeletal frame in her lap.
Her tears splashed against his parchment-like face,
evaporating like mist. His dark eyes widened as

though she was giving the gift of life back to him. A brief hope sprang up in Tamaika.

'No,' he wheezed, guessing what was in her mind. 'I am passing on.'

The noises were emanating from the level above them. Tamaika was torn between flight and helping the rift creature.

'I ... leave you a parting gift,' Odessar said.

'Lie still,' Tamaika said. 'You need help.'

'Not ... here,' Odessar said.

Two Hakogna pushed through the doorway.

Tamaika laid Odessar's head on the cold flags and brandished her sword. It seemed a feeble thing to do against such adversaries.

The Hakogna charged her. They were about to trample Odessar when the creature suddenly sat up and wove a complex sign in the air. As though struck by their own magic, the Hakogna suddenly froze, then stared about them, as if dazed. They looked at Tamaika, who hefted her sword, then together the two Hakogna bowed low to her and turned and left the chamber.

A pain-filled cry was wrenched from Odessar's lips and Tamaika rushed forward even as the creature collapsed back to the floor. No sooner had she reached him than a shimmering portal of pale green light materialised beside the still body.

Tamaika stood transfixed as the portal's light deepened to a forest green. Then it was as if a door had opened, showing a dark place within. Without conscious thought Tamaika lifted the wizened body and placed it within the cavity. At once a pearly light sprang up, engulfing the body. As the door closed she saw the creature's skin begin to renew itself and change. Then the portal shrank to a point of light and vanished with a soft popping noise, as though it had never been.

Tamaika stood for a long time, lost in thought, then eventually made her way from the chamber. Upstairs, the palace was in turmoil. Tamaika heard the Archon's strident voice demanding to know where his guards were. Staff were carrying debris and throwing it out into the grounds, others were tending the wounded and the dying. Already carpenters were restoring the palace doors. A dazed physician with a bloodied apron was walking aimlessly in circles.

There were no Hakogna to be seen.

Tamaika walked through the carnage, heedless of the occasional voice that demanded to know who she was. She passed the scullery maid whom she had saved earlier, but the girl seemed not to recognise her.

Guards had miraculously appeared at the main entrance. There seemed to be a lot of jostling and accusations going on, and then Tamaika saw Cador. His men were arresting some of the palace guards. He turned and saw her, and the next moment they were clenched tightly and kissing and laughing and crying, all at the same time.

'The Hakogna are gone, Tamaika,' Cador exclaimed. 'Just like that, they all returned to their rooftop perches,' he said. 'Turned back to statues.'

Tamaika smiled.

'And I've better news,' Cador said, pulling Tamaika aside. 'All those who were turned to stone …'

He stopped as Tamaika's hand flew to her mouth. Cador turned and saw a man standing in the broken entry. He was holding a book and was hugging it to his chest as if it were the most important thing he had ever found.

It was Tamaika's father and he seemed a little dazed.

'Tamaika?' he said.

A single sob escaped her, then she flung herself across the intervening space and into her father's arms, which embraced her with a fierceness she had almost forgotten.

'Forgive me everything,' he sobbed, his words muffled by Tamaika's hair. 'You're so like your mother I couldn't bear to look at you — her memory — it was too much for me.'

Tamaika hung on to him fiercely. 'Hush, Papa. Hush.'

Epilogue

QUENTARIS HAD SEEN MANY a celebration, although none quite surpassed those festivities held after the Hakogna Revolt, as those weeks became known.

Maxon was never found. Minstrels sang songs that told of an olive green light that opened up in the air and sucked Maxon into it, like a whirlpool at sea. Others held forth that Maxon escaped to plot his revenge. Although he had brought shame upon House Mercutis, Cador had more than earned the respect of Quentaris, and thus the House remained ennobled, fulfilling the promise Cador and his father had made to his mother.

Lord Chalm Eftangeny was said to muse that there were some strange parallels within this story: that Cador and Maxon were like day and night; that

Tamaika and Mithla were like chalk and cheese. He reflected too on the Hakogna, whose centuries-old fealty to Quentaris had been corrupted by an evil sorcerer as yet unaccounted for.

Cador — one of Quentaris's most eligible bachelors and now a prince of some means, publicly announced that he wished to marry the one true author of the city-wide bestseller, *Rift Enchantress*, Dacy Dunnard. A flurry of would-be authors came out of the woodwork, all claiming to be Dunnard.

Cador's father recovered from ill health and was his son's best man, while Tamaika's father escorted her down the aisle and gave her away. The grumbling sour-faced bridesmaids were Byra, Gabra and Hetta.

They fought like cats over the bridal bouquet.